REA

ACPL ITEM
DISCARDED

Fiction
Underwood, Michael   7030870
Double jeopardy

D0712149

DO NOT REMOVE
CARDS FROM POCKET

9-7-83

ALLEN COUNTY PUBLIC LIBRARY

FORT WAYNE, INDIANA 46802

You may return this book to any agency, branch,
or bookmobile of the Allen County Public Library.

DEMCO

DOUBLE JEOPARDY

by the same author

MURDER ON TRIAL
MURDER MADE ABSOLUTE
DEATH ON REMAND
FALSE WITNESS
LAWFUL PURSUIT
ARM OF THE LAW
CAUSE OF DEATH
DEATH BY MISADVENTURE
ADAM'S CASE
THE CASE AGAINST PHILLIP QUEST
GIRL FOUND DEAD
THE CRIME OF COLIN WISE
THE UNPROFESSIONAL SPY
THE ANXIOUS CONSPIRATOR
A CRIME APART
THE MAN WHO DIED ON FRIDAY
THE MAN WHO KILLED TOO SOON
THE SHADOW GAME
THE SILENT LIARS
SHEM'S DEMISE
A TROUT IN THE MILK
REWARD FOR A DEFECTOR
A PINCH OF SNUFF
THE JUROR
MENACES, MENACES
MURDER WITH MALICE
THE FATAL TRIP
CROOKED WOOD
ANYTHING BUT THE TRUTH
SMOOTH JUSTICE
VICTIM OF CIRCUMSTANCE
A CLEAR CASE OF SUICIDE
CRIME UPON CRIME

DOUBLE JEOPARDY

DOUBLE JEOPARDY

Michael Underwood [pseud.]

John Michael Evelyn

ST. MARTIN'S PRESS
NEW YORK

ALLEN COUNTY PUBLIC LIBRARY
FORT WAYNE, INDIANA

Copyright © 1981 by Michael Underwood
For information, write: St. Martin's Press,
175 Fifth Avenue, New York, N.Y. 10010
Manufactured in the United States of America

Library of Congress Cataloging in Publication Data

Underwood, Michael, 1916-
    Double jeopardy.

    I. Title.
PR6055.V3D6   1981   823'.914   81-8821
ISBN 0-312-21814-1   AACR2

7030870

CHAPTER 1

'Oh, do come! It's going to be a lovely party with just a few special friends. And I've told Adrian so much about you, Rosa, he's longing to meet you.'

Rosa Epton hadn't seen Philippa for twelve years; in fact, not since they had left school at the end of the same summer term, with promises of keeping in touch with one another. But not long afterwards Philippa Henderson, as she then was, had gone to South Africa with her parents. Rosa recalled that Mr Henderson had mining interests, which had taken him there. She also knew from their school magazine, which she still received regularly, that Philippa had returned to England and married someone called Adrian Carver about whom she had written to the editor of the magazine with pride and uninhibited enthusiasm.

Enthusiasm, Rosa recalled, had always been Philippa's hallmark and it seemed undimmed by the passage of years when they met unexpectedly in Kensington High Street on a bright Saturday morning about a fortnight before Christmas.

Philippa prattled away eagerly about Adrian and his important job in the City, about their two children, Robert and Rosemary, and about their grand riverside home near Richmond. After all of which she had enquired whether Rosa herself was yet married and had ended up by issuing a pressing invitation to her New Year's Eve party.

Rosa, who didn't much care for large parties, had hesitated, but had yielded when Philippa said it was going to be only a small gathering of select friends. She had made Rosa feel that it would spoil it for everyone if she said no, so she had said yes, though aware that she was almost certainly making the wrong decision. Nevertheless, she knew she would be intrigued to meet this paragon of a husband whom Philippa had married.

5

After this surprise encounter outside a supermarket, Rosa had found herself busy right up until Christmas Eve. As junior partner in Snaith and Epton, a firm of solicitors which specialised in criminal cases, she was in court virtually every day. The same went for her partner, Robin Snaith.

On Christmas Eve she drove down to the Herefordshire village of which her father was the rector. He was a widower in his early seventies, Rosa's mother having died ten years previously when Rosa was eighteen. For several years he had lived alone in the rambling rectory until, at his daughter's suggestion (indeed, she had organised the arrangement), he had taken in three students from a nearby agricultural college as lodgers. It was a continuing arrangement that worked satisfactorily from everyone's point of view, though as Rosa drove home that Christmas Eve, she recalled how her brother David, who was twelve years older than herself and who had lived in America for the past fifteen years, had lectured her from the other side of the Atlantic on her duty to keep house for their father and give up any idea of working in London. She had always been grateful to her American sister-in-law, Susan, whom she had not met at that time, who had written telling her not to let herself be browbeaten.

'Older brothers are very good at laying down the law for others,' she had written robustly. 'If I'd listened to mine, I'd never have married yours.'

Her father was standing at his study window as she turned into the drive. Overgrown laurel bushes brushed against her small Honda car as she parked near the front door.

'How nice to see you again, Rosa dear!' he said, coming out to greet her. 'Had a good journey?'

'Yes, thanks, daddy,' she said, as they embraced. She glanced up at the familiar facade with its flaking stone. 'How's everything here?'

'Nothing's changed.' They moved inside the house. 'I'll leave you to go up to your room while I put the finishing touches to my Christmas sermon. Incidentally, you'll come to midnight mass, won't you?'

'Of course I shall.'

6

'Good. I just thought you might be too tired after your long drive.'

Her father still tended to regard London as being as far away as China, despite the existence of high speed motorways.

Rosa went up to her bedroom. Somebody had thoughtfully switched on an electric fire; doubtless one of the ladies from the village who came in well organised relays to look after the rector's domestic needs. She had always occupied the same bedroom and could never enter it without a flood of childhood memories. As she now gazed round, she recalled a visit by Philippa during a summer holiday. The memory of that week was particularly clear, for after Philippa's departure, the rectory had seemed quieter than a morgue and it had taken her a whole day to re-adjust to her old routine.

With a brother twelve years older than herself and a mother and father who could almost pass for her grandparents, she had had a somewhat solitary upbringing. Not that this had ever bothered her. She had always been a self-reliant person, even as a small girl.

She unpacked and went downstairs to find her father in the kitchen standing over the kettle as if preparing to perform a miracle.

'I thought you'd like a cup of tea,' he said, as she entered.

'You go back to your sermon. I'll make the tea.'

'The sermon can wait,' he said with a sigh. 'I'm afraid it's not very inspired, anyway.'

Rosa, who had no high opinion of her father as a preacher, felt she ought to say something reassuring, but instead turned awkwardly away.

'I heard from David a few days ago,' he said, seizing the handle of the boiling kettle with a grimly determined expression. 'He's hoping to come over in the summer.'

'Just him or with Susan and the children?'

'All of them. I expect the children will want you to show them round London.'

'As long as David realises that I can't put them up.'

'Is your flat very small?'

'Tiny. Even looking after a neighbour's cat stretched its facilities.'

'But you're happy?' her father asked anxiously.

'I enjoy my work enormously.'

'Work isn't everything, Rosa.'

'Then let me say that I enjoy my whole life.'

'Some would say that a woman has to be married before she can be really fulfilled,' her father said in a gently chiding tone.

Rosa gave him her own version of the Mona Lisa smile, but said nothing. After all, it was Christmas Eve and she hadn't come all this way to start a quarrel. She was well aware that her father held old-fashioned views on the role of women in society, including a somewhat ambivalent one of his own daughter's career. He was proud of her achievement in becoming a solicitor, but was vaguely disapproving of the milieu in which she had chosen to practise. As an elderly parson who had spent all his life in the country, he deplored the wanton and vicious crime that went on in the big cities and was unable to understand how his daughter could find fulfilment defending such riff-raff. It was one thing to pray for their souls at a distance, quite another to try and snatch them from earthly retribution. To him practice of the law still conjured up a picture of dusty tomes and opinions written with quill pens.

'Do you remember a schoolfriend of mine called Philippa?' Rosa asked, deciding that a change of subject was required.

'Was she the one who never stopped talking?'

'Yes. I suddenly ran into her about two weeks ago. I hadn't seen her since we left school. She's invited me to a New Year's Eve party.'

'Are you going?'

'I've said I will, but am rather wishing I hadn't.'

'Why don't you want to go?'

'Laziness really. I find it an effort being sociable to people I'm never likely to meet again.'

'That's no way for a girl of your age to talk.'

'Perhaps not. Anyway, I am going.'

'You've obviously inherited your mother's reserve. She

8

always found meeting people something of a strain. But I'd have thought you'd get used to it in your work.'

'That's different.'

'I hadn't realised you were a shy person,' he persisted.

Rosa sighed and began to wish she hadn't changed the subject after all. The trouble was that she and her father seemed unable to talk for more than five minutes without ending up on opposite sides of a chasm.

'No, I'm not shy, but I'm also not terribly sociable. That's all I'm saying.'

Her father gave her a worried look. 'I've told some of the people in the village you're here for Christmas – well, they'd see you in church, anyway – and I'm sure they'd like a visit. The Nappers and the Rollenburys and old Mrs Vaisey who's virtually housebound nowadays.'

'Of course I'll go and see them,' Rosa said promptly. In fact, she always enjoyed her round of duty visits. These were people she had known all her life and with whom she felt completely at ease.

'How long will you be staying?'

'I must go back on Sunday. I'm in court the next day.'

'I thought the courts closed over Christmas and the New Year.'

'Not the ones I practise in. Not the magistrates' courts. They sit every weekday except Good Friday and Christmas Day.'

'Well I never,' he said abstractedly. 'I don't know why we've had tea standing up in the kitchen.'

'You'd better go and finish your sermon and I'll wash the cups.'

She watched him amble away. He had aged in the last two years, his step was not as firm as it had been, though his hair had been the same all the time Rosa could remember. It was still only partially grey, no sparser than twenty years previously and always as carefully brushed as that of a thirties matinee idol. But to Rosa he had always been an old man.

The next three days passed agreeably enough, but Rosa was not sorry when Sunday arrived.

9

'When'll you come again?' her father asked as they went out to her car.

'I'm not sure, daddy, but I'll keep in touch with you on the phone. Shall I give your regards to Philippa when I see her?'

'Oh, er, certainly,' he said after an abashed pause. 'And God take care of you, my child.'

Giving him a quick kiss, Rosa got into her car and, with a final wave, accelerated down the drive. When she reached the main road, a mile and a half out of the village, she let out a long sigh that summed up all her feelings about home.

For the next several miles she wrestled with her conscience about harbouring such feelings, then decided that the important thing was to go on making visits.

CHAPTER 2

There were cars parked up on the verge on both sides of the road.

'Are you for Mrs Carver's party, miss?' an old man asked, shining a torch through the window of Rosa's car.

She felt like saying 'no' and quickly driving on, but the old man obviously took an affirmative answer for granted.

'It's getting to be murder,' he said lugubriously. 'I don't know how I'm supposed to find a place for everyone and heaven forbid the police suddenly appearing.' He stood back and sized up Rosa's new Honda. 'I think I can fit you in over there, miss. I've been keeping one or two places near the house clear for specials like yourself.'

Rosa expressed her gratitude by handing him a fifty pence piece. She suspected he was probably making quite a good collection by use of this gambit.

Loud music poured forth from the house, which was floodlit and stood back from the road on the river side. Her heart sinking deeper with every step, Rosa walked up the tarmacked drive which was full of cars. Presumably the earlier arrivals.

She reached the porticoed front door and could hear voices on the farther side. Suddenly it opened and Philippa peered out.

'Rosa!' she exclaimed in an ecstatic tone. 'How lovely! Let me show you where to leave your coat! What a heavenly dress! And then you must meet Adrian if I can find him.'

They passed a long room which ran the breadth of the house and which appeared to be packed with people.

Philippa's few special friends clearly ran into over a hundred and presumably there were more to come.

Why on earth did I say 'yes', Rosa reflected gloomily as she laid her coat on a bed in one of the upstairs rooms. She studied

11

her unhappy reflection in the mirror and guessed she was probably the only woman present who had not been to the hairdresser that day. All she had done was wash it herself and give it an extra good brush. She wore her hair parted in the centre so that it hung evenly on either side of her elfin face. It had a habit of falling forward each time she bent her head. She had on a long emerald green dress with sleeves to the wrist and her only jewellery was a gold chain which had belonged to her mother and a pair of small jade earrings which Robin Snaith had given her to celebrate her becoming a partner in the firm.

Deciding that no further titivation was required, she went downstairs where the number of guests seemed to have further swelled. As she entered the room, an amiable-looking man of about forty handed her a glass of champagne.

'I'm Adrian Carver,' he said. 'I'm supposed to be the host at this do. I don't think we've met before.'

'I'm Rosa Epton.'

'So you're Rosa! I gather you and Philippa were a couple of giggling schoolgirls together. She's often mentioned you.'

'We didn't giggle all the time,' Rosa said with a smile. 'I remember once hitting Philippa with a hockey stick.'

'What I've sometimes felt like doing. Is it true that you're now a solicitor?'

'Yes.'

'You look much too young and fragile.'

'Perhaps I ought to have worn my black jacket and pin-stripes.'

'I'm sorry, I hope I wasn't rude.'

'You weren't. But I'm the same age as Philippa and, as to looking frail, don't be deceived by appearances.'

'Obviously not. Here, have another glass of champagne,' he said, waylaying a waiter who had just entered the room carrying a fresh bottle.

'I understood from Philippa that it was to be a small party,' Rosa said, glancing round the room.

'That *was* the intention, but my wife throws all caution to the winds when it comes to giving a party. She can't resist inviting everyone we've ever met, and on New Year's Eve a few more besides.' He gazed round the room with a detached air.

A woman with a horse-like face suddenly swooped up to them and clutched Adrian's arm. 'Adrian darling, you must come over and be introduced to my new husband.'

He gave Rosa a resigned look and she responded with a small wave as he allowed himself to be led away. She espied Philippa on the farther side of the room and decided to make her way across. Before she had time to move, however, a voice beside her spoke.

'Hello, have you lost your partner, too?'

She turned her head to see a chunky young man of about her own age eyeing her with a wry smile. He looked hot and was wearing black leather trousers and a pale lemon coloured shirt whose top buttons were undone to reveal an extremely hairy chest.

'As a matter of fact, I'm here on my own,' Rosa said. There was something rather engaging about her new companion. He had clear grey eyes and straight hair which fell across his forehead. 'What's happened to your partner then?'

'If you really want to know,' he said in a confidential tone, 'she's been behaving like a bitch the whole evening. She can be smashing, but she's as unpredictable as the weather. By the way, my name's Toby Nash.'

'Why'd you bring her?' Rosa enquired.

'I didn't. She brought me. She's a distant relative of Adrian Carver's. That is the name of the people who own this place, isn't it?'

'To the best of my knowledge and belief, yes.'

'You sounded just like a lawyer when you said that.'

'I didn't mean to, even though I am one. I must obviously watch my tongue, as legal phraseology can be the death knell to ordinary conversation.'

'Are you really a lawyer?' he asked with a surprised grin. 'What do you do, handle divorce cases and things like that?'

'No. My firm's practice is almost entirely in criminal courts.'

Toby shook his head in what appeared to be delighted surprise while continuing to grin at her.

'How do you get on with robbers and murderers?'he asked curiously, then hurriedly went on, 'O.K., don't say anything. I realise that was a bloody silly question. Incidentally, you've not told me your name.'

'Rosa. Rosa Epton.'

'Why don't we go and dance, Rosa?'

'If you're not worried about your girl-friend ... '

'Worried about her! For all I care she can be under the bushes outside with half a dozen men.'

Slipping an arm round Rosa's waist, he steered her toward open double doors beyond which was another room where dancing was taking place. She quickly discovered that, though he wasn't a polished dancer, he had a sense of rhythm and made up in energy what he lacked in skill.

'Let me try and guess what you do for a living,' she said, delicately moving her cheek away from his. 'I think you could work in television or possibly you're a travel agent.'

'Supposing I told you I was one of the top professional tennis players?'

'I shouldn't believe you, though now you mention it, you do bear a faint resemblance to Jimmy Connors.'

'I wish I earned his money.'

'So what are you?'

'I'm a merchant banker.'

'That sounds impressive.'

'Do you think so?'

'Much more than being a solicitor.'

'I don't mean I own a merchant bank.'

'I didn't think you did. Which bank are you with?'

'Prosser's.' He whirled Rosa across two yards of clear space. 'And to complete my life story, I share a flat in Swiss Cottage with someone called Sam.'

'Sam?'

'Samuel Brazier.'

'Ah!'

14

'You were wondering if Sam stood for Samantha, weren't you?'

'Well, it might have.'

'Sometimes it's useful to let people think it does. And where do you live, Rosa?'

'I've a small flat in Kensington.'

'Smart Kensington or down-at-heel Kensington?'

'Campden Hill.'

'Oh, very grand!'

'It's a minute flat.'

'And you live there alone?' he enquired, cocking his head on one side.

'Yes.'

They were dancing close to the double doors when Rosa was aware of a girl staring hard at her. She was attractive, even though her expression at that moment was not the most amiable.

'Would that be your girl-friend by any chance?' she whispered in Toby's ear.

He detached his cheek which he had once more placed against hers and glanced toward the door.

'Yes, that's Tricia. Do you mind if we move in her direction?'

'I think it'd probably be the wisest thing you could do.'

'Hi, Trish, this is Rosa Epton. And guess what, she's a lawyer.'

'I'm Tricia Langley,' the girl said to Rosa, ignoring Toby.

She was remarkably pretty, though her face seemed to lack any sign of animation. She resembled a girl on the front page of a fashion magazine. It was obvious from her immaculate appearance that she had not been rolling under any bushes; not even on top of a bed.

'Toby and I met when he was looking for you,' Rosa said tactfully. 'I return him undamaged. I gather you're a relative of Adrian's.'

'Our mothers are distant cousins. I suppose that means he and I are even more distant cousins. I've never bothered to work it out. Are you a friend of Philippa's?'

15

'We were at school together and happened to bump into each other just before Christmas. Incidentally, I must go and look for her. I've scarcely seen her since I arrived. Thanks for the dance, Toby. I'll probably see you both again later.'

She moved away quickly and returned to the other room where she spotted Philippa talking to an elderly couple and looking as if she would welcome escape. As she approached, Philippa gently propelled the couple toward the buffet and turned to greet Rosa.

'Rosa, darling, have you met everyone and are you all right?'

'I've talked to Adrian.'

'Isn't he gorgeous?'

'I thought he was very nice,' Rosa said emphatically.

'Oh, I'm so glad you liked him. Who else have you met?'

'Someone called Toby Nash.'

Philippa frowned. 'I'm sure I never invited anyone of that name.'

'He came with a cousin of Adrian's. Tricia Langley.'

'Oh, her! She's always got a different young man in tow. Once upon a time she used to get engaged to them, but she doesn't bother any more. Between you and me, I can't stand her. I only invited her out of habit.'

'What does she do?'

'She's a secretary. I must say I pity her boss.'

'She's probably very efficient.'

'I'd sooner have someone who spilt nail varnish on my letters and didn't look perpetually dissatisfied.'

'But you're not a man.'

Philippa laughed. 'You were always one for a wry comment, Rosa.' She glanced toward the buffet. 'Have you had anything to eat yet?'

'No.'

'Let me take you across to the food and then I must go and be nice to Adrian's boss and his dreary wife.'

'By the way,' Rosa said, 'my father sent you his regards. I spent Christmas at the rectory.'

'I'm sure he's never recovered from my visit,' Philippa

16

remarked with another burst of laughter. 'Darling, I must introduce you to somebody. Whom would you like to meet?' Before Rosa could reply, she had waylaid a passing male. 'Roger, you must meet Rosa Epton. She's one of my oldest friends.' Turning to Rosa, she said, 'This is Roger Trant. He works in Adrian's office. By the way, Roger, Rosa's a solicitor, so you'd better watch out.'

'Why should I do that?' Roger enquired with a puzzled expression as Philippa shot away.

'I've no idea.'

'I must say, you don't look like a solicitor,' he said.

'So I'm being constantly told,' Rosa replied wearily. 'On the other hand, you look exactly like someone who works in Adrian's office.'

Roger blinked. 'Do I?' He seemed to ponder this solemnly for a while, then said somewhat stiffly, 'If you'll excuse me, I was on my way to get my fiancée some food.'

Rosa watched him go without regret. The whole party was far removed from her idea of pleasure and she would much sooner have been at home. A glance at her watch told her that it was only just after eleven. She supposed she couldn't creep away before the New Year had been seen in and her heart sank at the prospect of spending another hour.

She wondered what midnight surprises Philippa had in store for her guests. She would certainly have planned something special; Rosa was quite sure of that.

About five minutes before midnight Adrian corralled all the guests into the main room and waiters went round refilling everyone's glass. A radio was switched on and as the chimes of Big Ben filled the room, a small boy dressed up as Old Father Time was thrust unwillingly into the room where he stood glowering like a cornered animal. Rosa presumed this was Robert, Philippa's son.

On the last stroke of midnight, a little girl (it had to be Rosemary, thought Rosa) whirled in like a small Margot Fonteyn and fluttered round the space which had been cleared in the centre of the room. She approached Old Father Time and gave him a hefty push toward the door. It caught him unawares

17

and he was about to retaliate vigorously when Philippa intervened and the party degenerated into an orgy of toasts and kisses.

'Thank God, that's over,' Rosa thought as she drifted away from the bearded young man who had been standing next to her and who had somewhat shyly kissed her on the cheek.

'I hope you don't mind,' he had said apologetically, 'but it seems to be the thing to do.'

Rosa had decided that any comment would only add to his embarrassment. She was about to go in search of Philippa to say her goodbyes when she noticed Toby and Tricia Langley standing in a corner of the room. Toby was gesticulating vehemently while Tricia was listening to him with a turned-down expression. It was clearly not the moment to approach them.

Rosa felt she could now decently leave and that was exactly what she proposed doing.

CHAPTER 3

New Year's Day being a public holiday, it was Rosa's intention to get up late and spend what was left of the morning giving her flat its first good clean since before Christmas. Then, depending on the weather, she would either go for a walk in Kensington Gardens or to the new French movie at the Curzon. The evening would have to be devoted to some work which she had brought home.

The office being closed for the day, she couldn't be pursued by phone calls. She would spare a thought, however, for her partner, Robin Snaith, who had a case in one of the magistrates' courts. She had, in fact, generously offered to do it for him, but he had declined, saying that a morning in court was preferable to one spent visiting his mother-in-law.

As so often when she went to bed late, she awoke early. It always seemed to happen on the occasions when there was no compelling reason to get up.

Nevertheless she found it agreeable to lie snugly warm in her tiny bedroom and listen to a few discordant sounds of life outside. She could hear drunken singing in the distance. Presumably a reveller still celebrating the arrival of a new year.

She had been awake about half an hour when the telephone on her bedside table rang.

'Is that Miss Rosa Epton?' a voice enquired.

'Yes.'

'This is Petersham police station, D.C. Fox, Miss Epton. I'm speaking on behalf of Detective Inspector Dormer. We have a prisoner who's appearing in court later this morning and who asked us to get in touch with you. His name's Nash. Toby Nash.'

19

'What's he charged with?' Rosa asked in her most professional voice.

'Rape.'

'Rape?' she cried out in astonishment.

'That's right. He'd like you to come to court and represent him, though I can't see it'll do him much good. It'll only be a formal appearance and we'll be asking for a week's remand.'

'Are you opposing bail?'

'Yes, we'll be asking for a remand in custody.' The voice hesitated. 'Inspector Dormer said to tell you that he's already spoken to the magistrates' clerk and doesn't anticipate any difficulty. So it's probably not worth your while attending.'

'Is that also part of Inspector Dormer's message?' Rosa asked in a steely tone.

'He just said to let you know the position,' said a now discomfited voice.

'Then perhaps you would kindly inform your D.I. and the clerk to the justices that I will certainly be there. And I shall be grateful if you will also let Mr Nash know. By the way, what time does the court sit?'

'Ten thirty. They've only got three short matters to deal with and I know they're hoping to complete their business quickly.'

'Thank you for telling me,' Rosa remarked drily. 'Whereabouts is the court situated? It's not one I know.'

'It's opposite the police station. You can't miss it.'

'I'll be there in good time.'

When Detective Constable Fox reported this conversation to his D.I., Dormer rounded on him.

'What the hell did you want to go and phone her at home for?'

'Because I didn't think her office would be open today, sir.'

'Too bloody right it won't be! So you had to go to all the trouble of running her to earth at home?' Dormer remarked in a tone of disgust.

'Yes, sir,' Fox said unhappily.

'Of all the bloody stupid things to do! Now we're all going to have to hang around until this woman arrives.'

'She said she'd be here in good time, sir.'

'She'd better be! Having been up all night, I don't intend waiting around for some tiresome female solicitor. I've a good mind to ask the magistrates' clerk to take the case first. Serve her right if she arrives to find her client's already on his way to Brixton prison.'

'She did ask, sir, that the clerk and Nash be told she was coming.'

Detective Inspector Dormer turned away fuming and D.C. Fox left the room with a sigh of relief, though he suspected there was worse to come.

When talking to D.C. Fox on the phone, Rosa had, for some reason she'd have found difficult to explain, shrunk from enquiring the name of the girl who had been raped. Her immediate assumption was that it must be Tricia Langley, but on further reflection, she rejected this as unlikely. What seemed more probable was that Toby and Tricia had had a final quarrel and that he had left the party with someone else. Or more likely still that he had left on his own and picked up some girl on his way home. In the mood he would have been in, this seemed quite feasible.

In Rosa's experience as a criminal lawyer, rape cases generally fell into one of two categories. The more rare were the cases of genuine rape where the victim had fought in vain to save her honour and had cuts and bruises and other injuries to support her story. But by far the more common case was that in which the girl had cried 'Stop' too late and it was left to a jury to decide at what stage she had withdrawn her consent.

As she drove down to Petersham Magistrates' Court, Rosa hoped that the case against Toby fell into this second category. When she arrived, she parked outside and walked across the street to the police station.

'What can I do for you, miss?' asked a uniformed sergeant in the general office.

'I'd like to see Detective Inspector Dormer.'

'Are you the solicitor representing Nash?' he said, looking at her with interest.

21

'Yes. If Mr Dormer's not available, I'd like to see my client. In fact, it might be better if I saw him first anyway.'

'I know the D.I. wants to have a word with you,' the sergeant said firmly. 'I'll let him know you're here.' He dialled an extension. 'Peter? Nash's solicitor has arrived. She's down here. Tell the D.I., will you?' Turning back to Rosa, he said, 'Just hang on a moment and somebody'll be down.'

Rosa heard footsteps on a staircase somewhere at the back and a few seconds later a young man came through a door into the enquiry office.

'Miss Epton? I'm D.C. Fox. We've spoken on the phone.'

'We have indeed.'

'Inspector Dormer's waiting,' he said nervously, 'I'll take you to his office.'

Rosa followed him up a flight of stairs and along an echoing corridor. Fox knocked on a door at the far end and opened it cautiously as if half-expecting to find it booby-trapped.

Slouched in a chair behind an untidy desk was a man in his mid-forties. His hair was rumpled and he stared at Rosa as if she was the last person he wished to see. His expression was uncompromisingly hard and he made no effort to get up.

'Are you proposing to represent Nash?' he asked with a sniff.

'I wouldn't have come here otherwise,' Rosa retorted.

'You do realise this'll only be a formal hearing? I'll be getting a week's remand in custody.'

'Getting?'

'Yes, getting. You haven't a hope of bail.'

'I shall still apply if my client wishes me to.'

'That's up to you, but I'm telling you it'll be a waste of time.'

'If that's all you have to say, I'd like to see my client immediately.'

'There is one further thing, Miss ... Hepton, is it?'

'Epton.'

'Miss Epton then. It's as well you should know that I'm not one of those police officers who gets ally pally with the defence.

22

So don't try and get any favours out of me, because you won't succeed!'

'I take it that also means you won't expect to get any out of me,' Rosa said with a note of challenge.

Inspector Dormer's scowl turned into an angry glare when he looked up and observed D.C. Fox's respectful glance in Rosa's direction. 'Take her down to see Nash,' he said, 'but don't be late bringing him across to court.'

'The D.I.'s feeling a bit rough,' Fox said as they made their way downstairs. 'He's been up all night.'

Rosa didn't believe for one moment that Dormer was any different even after a proper night's sleep. Her chief desire now was hearing from Toby exactly what had happened. For a charge of rape to have been brought so quickly after the offence must mean that the police were completely satisfied by the girl's story, and that she must have shown a determination to pursue the case. Except that with somebody like D.I. Dormer in charge one couldn't be certain of anything. Where a more circumspect colleague might hold back, he would plunge in.

As they reached Toby's cell, D.C. Fox said, 'Can I trust you, Miss Epton, not to give him anything?'

'Not even a cyanide capsule?'

'Not even a chocolate cigarette,' he said with a nervous laugh. 'You've seen what the D.I.'s like.'

'You needn't worry, I won't drop you in anything.'

Rosa experienced a moment of shyness as she entered the cell, but then her professional self took charge.

'Hello, Toby,' she said as he looked up from the bed on which he was sitting in an attitude of utter dejection.

He jumped to his feet, his expression transformed. 'Am I pleased to see you! I didn't know if you'd come.'

'I sent you a message saying I would.'

'That bastard Dormer pretended not to know whether you would or not.'

He was wearing a zip-up brown corduroy jacket over the familiar yellow shirt which now looked even more the worse for wear. He was unshaven and clearly in a state of considerable anxiety.

23

'You'd better tell me exactly what's happened,' Rosa said calmly. 'All I know so far is that you've been charged with rape.'

'It's crazy,' Toby said in an agitated voice. 'The whole thing's become a nightmare.'

'You can begin by telling me whom you're supposed to have raped.'

He looked at her in astonishment. 'Tricia, of course. Tricia Langley. Who else did you think it was?'

Rosa swallowed her own surprise. 'I just wanted to know,' she said weakly. 'Where did it happen?'

'In the car. I ask you, how can you rape anyone in a car? It's hard enough when they co-operate.'

Rosa had heard this argument often enough before. Certainly the back of a car was not the easiest place for a violent tangle of limbs.

'What sort of car?' she asked.

'A Ford Fiesta.'

'O.K., so you and Tricia left the party together, what happened after that?'

'It'd been a pretty rotten evening altogether. Tricia had been in a foul, bitchy mood and had kept on leaving me high and dry. Well, you remember, that's how we met. I didn't know anyone else there so I became increasingly narked by the way she was treating me. However, she seemed in a slightly better mood at the end.'

'What time did you leave?'

'Around two. There were still quite a few people keeping the party going, but she said she wanted to be taken home. Anyway, after about a mile I stopped the car a hundred yards or so up a private road that led to a sports ground and we started kissing. After a bit, I suggested we should get in the back and she was perfectly willing.' He let out a hollow laugh. 'The big deal at last, I thought at the time. Well, one thing led to another until she suddenly began making a fuss. She scratched my face and said I was trying to rape her and if I didn't stop immediately she'd tell the world the sort of person I was. I admit that I got a bit worked up at that point and I told her exactly what she

24

was, which wasn't very complimentary. I said it was usually the girls who cried rape who enjoyed it most. Anyway, I managed to have intercourse with her and when it was all over and we were back in the front of the car, she told me to drive her to the nearest police station. I asked her why and she said in her most infuriatingly superior tone, so that she could report me for rape. I was feeling thoroughly needled by her whole attitude, so I said, in a tone to match her own, certainly if that was what she wanted. To tell the truth, I was pretty sure I was calling her bluff. But when we arrived outside the police station, she marched inside. I must have sat in the car for about half an hour – I very nearly drove off and left her – when a couple of strong-arm officers appeared and told me to accompany them. They made it clear that I didn't have any choice in the matter. I was taken to a room where I was grilled by that man, Dormer. The rest you more or less know.'

'How long was it before you were charged?'

Toby shrugged helplessly. 'I've no idea. They kept on leaving me and coming back. I suppose they were interviewing Tricia in another room. I remember now that Dormer said they were waiting for a doctor to come and examine her.'

'Were you examined by a doctor, too?'

Toby hung his head as if in disgrace.

'Yes,' he said.

'That's what I'd have expected,' Rosa remarked with a small reassuring smile. 'Have the police taken possession of any of your clothing?'

He nodded. 'My vest and underpants. They said they'd also taken a rug from the back of the car.'

'Have you made a written statement?'

'I've told them the truth. I told them it was no more rape than a game of hopscotch is a heavyweight fight.' He gave Rosa a pleading look. 'You will be able to get me bail, won't you?' he said urgently.

'I'll do my best, but it's not going to be easy.'

'But I must have bail,' he wailed. 'I'm due back at work tomorrow.'

'Look, Toby,' she said, feeling like a parent speaking to a

25

distraught child, 'it's a serious charge and the police are going to ask for a week's remand in custody. In the circumstances, there's probably little I can say which'll persuade the magistrates to grant you bail today.'

He shook his head disbelievingly. 'Isn't there any other way of getting it?' he asked forlornly.

'One can apply to a judge in chambers.'

'Will you do that, if necessary?'

'Gladly,' Rosa said cheerfully. 'It probably won't succeed, but at least it'll put Inspector Dormer to a certain amount of inconvenience.' She glanced at her watch. 'You'll be going over to court shortly, but we'll have another talk afterwards. I'm afraid you must reconcile yourself to spending a week in Brixton prison. There'll be a better chance of getting bail next time.'

It didn't require a second glance to see that the magistrates' court on New Year's Day was far from being a public attraction. The clerk gave Rosa a suspicious glance as she took her seat. D.I. Dormer had undoubtedly warned him that she was a troublemaker.

When Toby's case was called and he was ushered into court, Dormer stepped briskly into the witness box and announced that he would like a week's remand in custody as the police had many further enquiries to make. He added that the gravity of the charge warranted his application. He addressed the magistrates in a tone that suggested their decision was a foregone conclusion.

When he had finished, the clerk turned to Rosa and said in a resigned tone, 'Do you wish to ask the inspector any questions?'

'One or two,' Rosa said, getting to her feet and turning to face Inspector Dormer who had assumed a stony look. 'Is it a fact that the accused himself drove the complainant to the police station?'

'So I understand.'

'And then sat outside in his car until your officers fetched him in?'

'Yes.'

'From that, would you agree that he doesn't sound like someone who'll abscond if granted bail?'

'No.'

'You mean that you don't agree?'

'Precisely.'

'Why not?'

'Now that he's been charged, the temptation to abscond will be stronger.'

'You're aware that he has a fixed address and holds a responsible position in a bank?'

'So he says.'

'Don't you believe him?'

'I've not been able to check anything he's told me. The bank is closed today and there's no answer from his flat.'

'If substantial sureties can be found, do you still oppose bail?'

'Yes.'

'Do you agree that rape can vary enormously in its heinousness?'

'As far as I'm concerned, rape is rape and one of the most serious charges known to the criminal law.' As he spoke, Inspector Dormer glanced round the court-room with an air of triumph.

Rosa indicated that she had no further questions to ask and began addressing the magistrates, all three of whom had pleasant, attentive expressions. Even so, with their clerk and a senior police officer ganged up against her, she knew she stood small chance of succeeding in her plea.

Fixing the chairman with a firm gaze, she said, 'I know, sir, that you won't just rubber-stamp Detective Inspector Dormer's application for a remand in custody, but will wish to consider the facts and merits of the matter.'

For a full five minutes she argued with considerable persuasion why Toby should be granted bail. She felt that, if she could have addressed the magistrates privately, she might have won them over. As it was, however, they were inevitably going to take the soft option, particularly when their clerk advised them it was a perfectly reasonable application on the

27

part of the police. A week's remand in custody wasn't going to harm anyone, it would be said. At worst, it would be a minor inconvenience to this young man in the dock, who had, after all, brought the whole thing on his own head. Let him out on bail at this stage against police wishes and heaven knows what dire consequences could ensue. He might never be seen again or, worse still, run amok every night of the week.

When Rosa resumed her seat, the clerk turned to D.I. Dormer and remarked, 'If the accused were to be granted bail, is there a danger he might interfere with witnesses?'

'Yes, I think that's a distinct possibility, sir,' Dormer said with a complacent nod.

Rosa shot to her feet. 'I don't know why your learned clerk thought fit to make that tendentious suggestion,' she said indignantly. 'There's no evidence to support it and my client would be quite willing to give an undertaking that he will not communicate with the complainant or any other witness.'

The magistrates looked non-plussed, like firemen caught without any water. However, their clerk turned round and whispered to them, after which the chairman announced that they would retire to consider their decision.

'Why the hell do they need to retire?' Dormer asked the clerk after they had withdrawn.

The clerk shrugged. 'Justice must always be seen to be done,' he remarked with a small cynical smile. 'But I'm sure you needn't worry.'

'I should bloody well hope not.' He turned away and ostentatiously ignored Rosa as he walked past where she was sitting.

A few minutes later the three magistrates returned to court and the chairman addressed Toby.

'We have decided that you will be remanded in custody for one week.' Glancing in Rosa's direction, he said in a tone that pleaded for understanding, 'We'll certainly be ready to reconsider the matter next week, Miss Epton, if you renew your application.'

With Inspector Dormer frowning ominously, Rosa hurried

out of court to console Toby. He looked as forlorn as she expected and she decided to be briskly practical.

'I'm sorry we weren't successful, but I think there's every chance you'll get bail next week.'

'I thought you said you could appeal to a judge,' he remarked gloomily.

'Yes, but don't pin too many hopes on that. I'll certainly try though ... '

'When?' he broke in.

'Either tomorrow or the next day, depending on how soon I can do the necessary paper work. Meanwhile, there are some other matters we must discuss. First of all, I'll arrange for your car to be collected from the police station. It can probably be parked outside my flat if you're prepared to risk that.' He nodded abstractedly. 'The next thing is, I imagine you'd like me to ring your flat-mate, Sam, and tell him what's happened to you?'

'I suppose you'd better. He'll be back this evening.'

'And what about the bank? What are they to be told?'

'Sam knows my boss. Perhaps he could call him and say I've had an accident,' Toby said miserably.

'Can Sam be trusted to make up a good story?'

'He's a copy-writer in an advertising agency,' Toby remarked, as if this fully answered the question.

'Incidentally, what exactly is your position at the bank?'

'I'm just a clerk. It's a deadly dull job and I usually make it sound a bit better by saying I'm a merchant banker.' He gave Rosa a rueful smile.

She gave a small laugh. 'Just like the barrow boys who describe themselves as company directors.' Her eyes focused on his shirt. 'I'd better bring you a change of clothes when I come and see you in Brixton in a few days time. I can liaise with Sam about that. It might be a good idea to wear one of your office suits and put on a tie when you appear in court next week. I take it you do wear a tie at the bank?'

'It's about the only place I do.' He gave her an anxious look. 'Will you be getting in touch with Tricia? Make her see what a ghastly mistake she's made.'

29

'I can't do that, Toby. She's now a prosecution witness. *The* prosecution witness and it would be unethical for me to have any contact with her.'

'Somebody must talk sense into her,' Toby said urgently. 'Ask Sam to phone her!'

'If Dormer gets wind that you're trying to nobble his chief witness, you really will be in trouble. I'm afraid you must dismiss that notion from your mind. Incidentally, where does she live?'

'She shares a flat in Fulham with two other girls, Sara and Janice. I don't know their other names. The address is Flat 4, 52 Fillery Street.'

'Does she have a job? I remember now, she's a secretary, isn't she?' Observing Toby's surprised expression, she added, 'Philippa told me.'

'Philippa?'

'Your hostess of last night if you've forgotten. How long have you known her?'

'I first met her through a cousin of mine called Peter Rossington. He and Tricia were engaged until she threw him over ... '

'Because of you?'

'Good grief, no! She just became bored with him. But poor old Peter took it very badly. Went off his food and eventually lost his job. Tricia and I have only been out a few times together. I never cared for her very much, even before this.'

'Why do you go out with her then?'

'Good question! I suppose because I seldom say "no" to anything. Moreover, she's attractive and can be fun when she's in the right mood.' He gave Rosa another small rueful smile. 'To tell the truth, I was rather chuffed when she invited me to go with her to the Carvers' party.'

After a pause, Rosa said with a slight air of embarrassment, 'There is one more question I ought to ask you about her. Was she a virgin?'

'Definitely not. But she was also nothing like as experienced as she pretended to be.' He flashed Rosa a hesitant look. 'She's what my father used to call a cock-teaser, if you know what I mean.'

'I know exactly what you mean. Had you had sex with her previously?'

He shook his head. 'No. I know it took Peter a fair old time before he could get her into bed. But he made it in the end.'

'I may need to talk to Peter, so you'd better give me his address.'

'He's been on the move recently, but you'll find his latest telephone number in my address book which is somewhere in the flat. Probably in my bedroom.'

The cell door opened and a uniformed sergeant appeared.

'Excuse me,' he said with a grin, 'but your limousine awaits.'

'He means the vehicle to take you to Brixton,' Rosa explained when Toby looked uncomprehending. 'Now don't worry, I'll be looking after things and I'll see you in a few days time.'

'May I take you out when this is all over?' he asked earnestly as he turned to go.

'It's a date,' Rosa said promptly.

Eighteen hours earlier she had never even heard of Toby Nash, now she had become more entangled in his life than she cared to admit.

On leaving the court-house, she walked across to the police station and asked for Detective Inspector Dormer.

'I'm afraid he's gone home,' D.C. Fox said, appearing in the entrance lobby.

'Then perhaps you'll inform him that I shall be applying for bail to a judge in chambers. It'll probably be either tomorrow afternoon or the next morning.'

D.C. Fox seemed to go pale. 'The D.I. was proposing to take leave the next two days,' he said anxiously.

'That's all right, if he's not there to oppose it, we'll get it by default,' Rosa said crisply.

'You couldn't postpone it until the day after?'

'Not without doing your D.I. a favour and I know he wouldn't expect that.' Observing Fox's anguished expression,

31

Rosa went on, 'I'm sorry for *you*, Mr Fox, but I'm afraid my client's interests come first.'

CHAPTER 4

On her way back into London, Rosa decided to call at the office which was not far from Hammersmith Broadway. It wasn't a fashionable area, but solicitors in criminal practice were rarely to be found in high class districts.

There would be nobody there, and she could spend a couple of quiet hours preparing the documents for the bail application.

She hadn't been at her desk for long, however, before she heard a key turn in the lock of the outside door.

'Is that you, Robin?' she called out.

'Is this your idea of how to spend New Year's day?' he asked, appearing in the doorway of her room. He dropped his briefcase on to the floor and came over and flopped down in the chair used by clients. 'What on earth's brought you in? You don't even have the excuse of a mother-in-law to avoid.'

While Rosa related the events of the previous evening and their aftermath, Robin sat back and listened attentively, his eyes seldom leaving her face.

Rosa had originally been his clerk, but had shown such an aptitude for the law that he had encouraged her to take her solicitor's exams. Once she had qualified, he had lost no time in offering her a partnership, a decision he had never for a single second regretted. She had, in his view, but one chink in her professional armour, namely a tendency to become emotionally involved with some of her clients. It didn't happen often, but it always caused Robin disquiet when he detected the signs. The clients who had the unsettling effect were always males in their twenties, but, that said, they were liable to come from any walk of life. Fortunately, her good sense had so far saved her from making a fool of herself and Robin prayed that it would always continue to do so.

It was apparent to him, as he now listened to her, that Toby Nash was the latest in this line. Moreover he had the distinction, if that was the right word, of being the first rapist in the list. He had noticed that it was invariably somebody who managed to excite Rosa's maternal streak. From her account of him, Toby emerged as an engaging, unconventional, cuddly, teddy-bear of a person. Robin couldn't help speculating, however, whether the other side of the coin might not reveal the picture of a fickle, dishonest and immoral young man.

'Is it going to embarrass you defending him?' he asked when she had finished speaking.

'I don't think so. Why?' she said a trifle militantly.

'I just wondered, that's all. It occured to me that having met him socially, danced with him and all that, you might feel uncomfortable about defending him on this particular charge.'

Rosa appeared to ponder this before answering. Then she said, 'If I do, Robin, I'll let you know.'

'Right. Well, I'll leave you to draft your bail application, though I doubt whether it'll bring you any joy.'

'It'll bring me joy all right,' she remarked, 'if only because it's going to annoy one of the rudest and most abrasive police officers I've ever come across.'

Robin Snaith grinned. Rosa might appear small and elfin, but it was an unwise police officer who thought he could trample over her. There were one or two who still bore scars from such encounters.

It was six o'clock by the time she got back to her flat and she immediately ran a bath. There was nothing like a long hot soak for relaxing both body and mind.

She had just got out and was in the process of drying herself when her telephone rang.

'Is that Rosa Epton?' a female voice enquired. It sounded vaguely familiar though she was unable to place it immediately.

'Yes, speaking.'

'This is Tricia Langley. We met at last night's party, though it seems much longer ago than that. I hope you don't mind my calling you?'

'Before you go on, are you aware that I'm representing Toby?'

'That's why I'm phoning you. The whole thing's got out of hand. It's awful what's happened.'

'What exactly are you trying to tell me?' Rosa asked cautiously.

'That I never meant Toby to be sent to prison ... '

'He's been remanded in custody for one week.'

'Yes, I know. I feel terrible about it.'

'We must be very careful what we say to each other, Tricia. If the police knew that you'd been in touch with me, they'd blow up. You're their chief witness and I'm in the opposite camp.'

'But I don't want to be a witness. I don't want to get Toby into further trouble.'

'I take it,' Rosa said, picking her words with care, 'that you've made a statement to the police and told them that you'd be prepared to give evidence against Toby?'

'I was so upset and angry at the time that my only thought was to spite him.'

You certainly did that all right, Rosa reflected. Aloud she said, 'Are you telling me there was no rape?' And held her breath as she waited for the answer.

'Toby was beastly and he hurt me – physically, I mean – but I never intended things to get this far.'

'But didn't you realise he was likely to be charged as a result of your allegation?'

'I tell you I was angry and upset and I just wanted to get my own back on him. I never dreamt he'd be kept in custody.'

'So what are you proposing to do about it?'

'What do you think I should do, Rosa?'

'I think you should call the police and tell them what you've told me.'

'You mean, tell them I don't want to go on with the case.'

'Yes, if that is your decision,' Rosa said cautiously.

The trouble was that she knew so little about Tricia Langley and what she did know wasn't very reassuring. There was

35

always the danger that, under police pressure, she might reverse her decision and even blurt out that Rosa had sought to influence her. In those circumstances, Rosa could envisage D.I. Dormer reacting venomously as far as she was concerned. He would be capable of conducting the sort of vendetta the Mafia would be proud of.

'As I've already said, Tricia,' she now went on, 'we're on opposite sides and I have to be careful not to say anything to influence you.'

That should sound all right if anyone's listening in, she reflected with a grim little smile.

'Will the police be upset if I tell them I don't wish to go on with the case?'

'From what I know of Inspector Dormer, the answer is very.'

'Can they do anything to me?'

Rosa sighed as she felt herself being sucked ever closer to a whirlpool.

'There is a criminal offence of making a false report and thereby wasting police time ... '

'But it wasn't a false report. Well, not exactly. Toby did force himself on me. The doctor could see I'd been hurt.'

'I really don't think we ought to talk any more,' Rosa said hastily. 'Why don't you consult your own solicitor about your position?'

'I don't have a solicitor of my own and my father's would die of shock if I told him. Oh God, what a mess it all is!' she exclaimed with a note of petulance.

'And all your fault, too,' Rosa reflected as she put down the receiver. Of one thing she was quite sure, D.I. Dormer wouldn't let the case slither away without putting up a fight. But if Tricia stuck to her guns, there was nothing he, or anybody else, could do about it.

Meanwhile, she had better get on with more immediate matters. She decided to find out if Sam Brazier had arrived back at the flat he shared with Toby.

'If you like, I'll go and collect his car,' Sam said promptly, after Rosa had explained what had happened.

'That would be terribly kind. Perhaps you could stop by here and bring me his address book and some of his clothes.'

'Certainly, I can do that.'

'If I may say so,' Rosa said, after they had discussed further details, 'you don't sound too surprised at the trouble Toby's landed in.'

Sam gave a laugh. 'I suppose I don't. That's because Toby's been constantly in and out of scrapes.'

'This is rather more than a scrape.'

'Yes, but Toby's always lived a fairly lusty sexual life.'

'You're not suggesting he's been charged with rape before?' Rosa asked anxiously.

'No, but there's always the risk with Toby, particularly with frigid sexpots like Tricia Langley.'

'I've never heard of anyone being both frigid and a sexpot.'

'In the same way you can burn your hand on a lump of frozen metal.'

'How well do you know her?' Rosa asked, after a thoughtful pause.

'As well as I want to. I warned Toby against her after she had discarded his cousin, Peter, as if he were an old Christmas card. Anyone could see that she spelt trouble for someone like Toby. But I'm afraid he's a bit of a hungry mongrel.'

'I see,' Rosa said in a hollow voice, feeling as if she had just received a ducking.

'Mind you,' Sam Brazier went on, 'he's still my best mate.'

'He'd like you to ring his boss at the bank and make some excuse for his not coming in this week. Can you do that?'

'It won't be the first time I've performed that service,' Sam said cheerfully. 'I'd better think up a really artistic one this time.'

Rosa felt as if she had just completed a circuit of the big dipper by the time she rang off. Talking to Sam Brazier had left her distinctly weak at the knees.

She slumped into an armchair and concentrated her mind furiously on the professional requirements of the case.

Before she went to bed, she telephoned her father to wish him a happy New Year.

37

CHAPTER 5

'Tricia's going to be late for work,' observed Sara Fitch, one of her flat-mates. 'Again,' she added.

'She's not working today,' replied Janice Turnbull. 'I've just put my head round her door. She's still in bed.'

'Is she still suffering from a New Year's Eve hangover?' Sara enquired.

Janice and Sara had been friends long before Tricia came into their lives. They had wanted a third person to share the expenses of their flat and Tricia (a friend of a friend of a friend) had presented herself. It was an arrangement that worked satisfactorily, primarily because Tricia had never made any effort to thrust her friendship on the other two.

'If she's going to be here all the morning,' Sara went on, 'she can take the rent down to nosy Norm. It'll spare us a visit from him when we get back this evening.'

Norman Oliver, their landlord, lived in the basement flat and was generally regarded as a creep.

After a pause Sara went on, 'Perhaps she is genuinely ill for once. I thought she looked rotten when I saw her yesterday. Ought we to find out if she needs anything?' But, when asked, Tricia said no thank you, she'd be all right and she would certainly deal with the rent.

'If Norm ever starts pawing her, he'll get frostbite,' Sara observed, as she and Janice left the house.

As soon as they had gone, Tricia put a call through to her office and spoke to Joyce Wyngard who was the firm's cashier and had been one of its pillars for twenty-five years.

'This is Tricia, Joyce. I'm afraid I shan't be in today. Will you tell Mr Harris?'

'Not coming in! What's wrong with you?' Joyce asked in her forthright manner.

38

'I'm not feeling very well.'

'Probably none of us is. But you had yesterday to get over your New Year's Eve excesses. That's why January the first has been made a public holiday. The government bowed to the inevitable.'

'It's nothing to do with excesses,' Tricia replied tartly.

'What *is* wrong with you then?' Without waiting for an answer, she went on, 'Your trouble, Tricia, is that you don't get enough exercise and fresh air. I'm over twice your age, but I'm far fitter than you are.'

Joyce Wyngard seldom missed an opportunity of sermonising about physical fitness and of boasting about all the classes she attended to maintain this desirable state.

'That's your trouble, it really is,' she repeated vigorously.

'If you're not very careful, I'll tell you what yours is,' Tricia said, rudely.

'Mine? What do you mean?' Joyce sounded oddly flustered.

'Just think about it, Joyce, that's all! Meanwhile tell Mr Harris I'm sorry, but that I'll hope to be in tomorrow.'

When she lifted the receiver to make her next call, Tricia was aware that her hand was trembling badly and it was with a sense of reprieve that she heard the flat doorbell ring.

'A happy New Year to you, Miss Langley,' said their landlord with an ingratiating smile as she opened the door. 'I thought I'd better come up and see if you were all right.' Before she could reply, he had stepped inside. 'I saw Miss Fitch and Miss Turnbull leave, but not you. I wondered if you might be unwell.'

'I'm quite all right. It's just that I'm not working today,' Tricia said, taking a step back after he had moved closer to her. 'But as you're here, I can give you the rent. I was going to bring it down later.'

He followed her into the sitting-room and brushed his hand against her thigh in doing so.

'Why don't we start the new year by exchanging first names?' he said with another ingratiating smile. 'I know you're Tricia and I'm Norman to my friends.'

And nosy Norm to your tenants, Tricia wanted to say. What

a horrid little man he was! She didn't really mind what he called her or what she called him, so long as their personal contact could be kept to a minimum.

She reached out for an envelope which was propped against a vase on the table.

'Here's the rent,' she said.

He took the envelope from her and contrived to stroke her hand.

'I expect you have lots of boyfriends, don't you?' he said with a faint leer.

'That's my business. I have no wish to discuss my private life.'

'No, of course not. And I'm the last person who'd want to pry. But I've always taken a personal interest in my tenants. Luckily, I've always got on with people, though I don't mind telling you, Tricia, you have to be broad-minded running a house like this. But my motto's always been, what the tenants get up to is their own business as long as they don't damage the fittings and are regular with the rent.' He gave a little chuckle while Tricia remained stony-faced. 'As I'm up here, perhaps I might check the sashcord in the small bedroom? Last time I looked, it appeared a bit frayed.' He hovered before her with a hopeful smile.

'It's perfectly safe and quite all right,' Tricia said firmly.

'Nevertheless, if it's not inconvenient ... '

'It is,' she broke in. 'It's my room and it's in a mess and I'd sooner you didn't go in.'

'Oh, you have that room, do you?'

'I think you know that perfectly well,' she said coldly.

Observing her implacable expression, the landlord decided to accept defeat for the moment.

'Well, if it's not convenient I won't press the matter, though I would be acting within my rights. I don't know if you've read the tenancy agreement.' At this point, however, he found himself addressing an empty room. He went out into the hall where Tricia was standing beside the open front door. 'I look forward to another little chat soon, Tricia,' he said cheerfully. 'I'll need to check on your bathroom heater in the next few days.

I gather it's been giving you a bit of trouble. Temperamental things, they are!' He put out a hand and rested it on Tricia's shoulder as though to console her for her ailing heater, but quickly removed it on observing her expression.

With his departure, Tricia returned to the telephone and again braced herself to make a call to the Petersham police.

D.I. Dormer had said he would be in touch with her before the next hearing and had told her not to hesitate to call him should anything arise to worry her. He had specifically warned her against interference from any of Toby's friends and had forecast dire consequences for them if this happened.

'May I speak to Inspector Dormer?' she said when a voice answered.

'He's not here today. Will anyone else do?'

'Is Woman Constable Jordan there?'

'No, she's out on a job. Who is it speaking?'

'Patricia Langley.'

'Is that the Miss Langley in the rape case?'

'Yes.'

'Hold on a moment. I'll put you through to Detective Constable Fox. He knows all about it.'

'D.C. Fox speaking,' a voice said a few moments later. 'Is that Miss Langley?'

Tricia felt suddenly unable to talk. It was like having climbed up to the highest diving board and becoming paralysed on looking down at the water.

'Are you there, Miss Langley?'

'Yes, I'm here,' she said in a dull tone.

'I gather you wanted to talk to somebody?'

'Yes.'

'Has anything happened?'

'No.'

'What is it you wanted to say?'

'I didn't really want to say anything, I just thought I'd phone.'

There was a pause before Fox spoke once more. 'Are you sure nothing's happened?' he asked in a worried voice.

'No, nothing. I'm fine.'

41

'That's good,' he said, though his tone was still puzzled.

'I hope I haven't wasted your time.'

'Think nothing of it, Miss Langley. As long as everything's all right, nothing else matters. I'll tell Inspector Dormer that you called. Would you like me to pass on any particular message?'

'No, thank you.'

'He'll probably call you as soon as he's back in the office. We do have your phone number, don't we?'

'Yes, but I'd sooner you didn't ring me here. The girls I share a flat with don't know what's happened. I haven't told them.'

'Can we ring you at your place of work, if necessary?'

'Preferably not. Nobody there knows either.'

'I see. Well, I'll make a note of that,' Fox said, though aware that his D.I. was unlikely to take the slightest notice. Indeed, he couldn't help wondering what Inspector Dormer's reaction to Tricia's call was likely to be. He would either dismiss it as neurotic or tear strips off Fox for not having done more about it. But Fox was unable to see what more he could do. His own view was that Tricia had become suddenly fearful like a child waking up in a strange room in the dark. In which event the very act of telephoning would have had a calming effect. Although he had given her every opportunity of saying why she had called, he was left feeling puzzled and even faintly disturbed when she rang off.

As for Tricia herself, she put down the telephone with a feeling of anti-climax. She told herself that there was still time to retract her complaint and even became persuaded that the moment could be deferred until she was actually in the witness box. That would be dramatic, all right! However, that might mean Toby being kept in custody for longer and she felt he had already been taught a sufficient lesson. She was genuinely horrified by what she had set in train, though this didn't mean she was eager for an act of reconciliation. Far from it, she wanted nothing further to do with Toby Nash once this mess was resolved.

She stared across the room with a distant expression. If only she had not acted so impulsively, she would never have landed herself in this ugly situation. In one sense, of course, it was all Toby's fault.

She recalled various things she'd heard and read about trials for rape. It seemed as if the complainant often had a worse time than the accused and ended up by being publicly humiliated. That was yet another reason for retracting her complaint earlier rather than later.

One moment she felt remorseful about Toby: the next she hated him for being another aggressively randy male.

CHAPTER 6

The application for bail to the Judge in Chambers had been unsuccessful, as Rosa had known it would be. The judge had been attentive and courteous before announcing that he felt the application to be premature. The magistrates, in refusing bail, had exercised their discretion and he was not disposed to interfere at this very early stage of proceedings. He had then thanked everyone for their attendance and they had shuffled out into the crowded corridor.

Rosa, who had never expected a different result, had the satisfaction of noting Inspector Dormer's expression of angry resentment. He studiously avoided speaking to her and she made no attempt to approach him. She longed, however, to know whether Tricia Langley had yet been in touch with him. One way or another she must try and find out before Toby's next appearance in court.

As soon as she returned to her office she decided to call Peter Rossington's number again. She had tried several times already without getting any reply. On this occasion a somewhat melancholy voice answered.

'Is that Peter Rossington?' she asked.

'Yes, who is that?'

'My name's Rosa Epton. I'm phoning about your cousin, Toby Nash. I'm his solicitor. Have you been in touch with him recently?'

'Not since before Christmas. Why?'

'Then I take it you're unaware that he's been charged with rape?'

'I'd no idea. When did this happen?'

'Two days ago. Would it be possible for us to meet and have a talk?'

'I don't see why not. When and where do you suggest?'

'Could you come to my office this afternoon? It's near Olympia.'

'All right.'

'Would three o'clock suit you?'

'O.K. What's the address?' After Rosa had told him, he said, 'By the way, who's Toby raped?'

'I'll tell you the whole story when I see you,' Rosa said quickly and rang off.

Peter Rossington's voice had sounded flat and sombre and Rosa tried to imagine what he would look like. She pictured a tall, gaunt, bespectacled young man with dark hair.

In the event, though he was somewhat gaunt in appearance, he wasn't particularly tall, nor did he wear spectacles. Moreover his hair was sandy in colour and starting to go thin. And his mouth, which she had pictured as a thin line, was full-lipped.

'Do sit down,' Rosa said, indicating her client's chair, after they had shaken hands. 'I'm afraid this may come as rather a shock to you, Mr Rossington, but the girl involved in the case is Tricia Langley.'

For several seconds he just blinked at her. Then he said quietly, 'I see.'

'I believe you were engaged to her at one time?'

'She broke it off. At one fifteen a.m. on Friday, August the thirtieth, to be precise,' he added with a small bitter smile. 'I was taking her home after a party and had just pulled up outside her house. Did Toby tell you I had a nervous breakdown as a result?'

'He said you'd been very upset.'

'*Been*? I'm still upset. I think of her all the time. And when I'm asleep, she haunts my dreams.' He gave Rosa a mournful look and said, as if the words had turned sour in his mouth, 'So Toby's raped Tricia! What else is new?'

'He says he didn't rape her,' Rosa remarked firmly.

'Toby's always been a randy little stoat.'

'I was going on to say that he alleges she consented to what took place.'

Peter Rossington gave a mirthless laugh.

45

'He says that she wasn't a virgin,' Rosa added, giving him an enquiring look.

He shook his head in a bemused way. 'Little did I think I'd be discussing all our sex lives when I came to see you.'

'I'm sorry if you find all this embarrassing, but I need to find out everything I can about Tricia. Can you confirm that she isn't a virgin?'

The question seemed to cause him considerable thought and his lips moved, as if in silent prayer, before he spoke. Eventually he said in a brittle tone, 'If Toby says she wasn't, why ask me?'

'Because if Tricia went into the witness box and said she had never had sex with anyone before, it would obviously assist Toby's case enormously to be able to prove that she was lying.'

'You can't expect me to get involved in all this,' he said in a suddenly harsh voice.

'I thought you'd want to help Toby if you could.'

'I don't know what I wish,' he said, shaking his head in an agitated fashion. 'I think I'd better go.'

Rosa watched him get up and dash for the door as though he was going to vomit. She made no attempt to stop him. It had not been a fruitful interview and she had learnt very little, save that he was an emotional and unstable young man.

She would need to ask Toby more about him when she visited Brixton prison the next day.

Ordinarily, she viewed visits to Brixton with as much enthusiasm as those to the dentist. The journey through South London was always appalling and the prison itself, when eventually reached, reduced her spirits to their lowest ebb.

On this occasion, however, she found herself looking forward to her visit with feelings that were more mixed than usual. She couldn't help experiencing a faint anticipatory tingle at the thought of seeing Toby again, though this was somewhat offset by the prospect of finding him in a state of black despair.

As she waited for his arrival in the interview cubicle, she pondered a variety of ways in which to greet him. Before she had come to any decision, she saw him through the glass

46

partition which separated the cubicle from the general area where prison staff maintained a watchful eye on everything that was going on. At the sight of the familiar lemon shirt, her heart gave a tiny flutter. A moment later, he was escorted into her presence.

He was looking surprisingly spruce (the lemon shirt apart) and greeted her with a cheerful grin.

'Welcome to my prison,' he said. 'It's already beginning to feel quite familiar. Not that I wish to stay longer than I have to. They told me my bail application was turned down.'

'I did warn you that it didn't stand much chance.'

'I know. Do you think the magistrates will really give me bail next time?'

'I very much hope so. Incidentally, I've brought you a change of clothes.'

'Good! This shirt's beginning to look and smell like something off the refuse heap.'

'You look pretty well, yourself,' Rosa said with an approving nod.

'We Nashes are like rubber balls. We usually bounce back fairly quickly. Did you speak to Sam?'

'Yes. He said he'd call your boss at the bank and say you'd be away for at least a week.'

'What was he going to tell him?'

'I didn't ask. He said he'd think of something and that it wouldn't be the first time.'

'Sam's a good friend,' Toby said in an appreciative tone.

'I had a phone call from Tricia,' Rosa said and went on to relate the conversation they'd had, while Toby listened intently.

'Does that mean she's dropping the case?' he asked eagerly.

'Technically it's not hers to drop.'

'But how can it possibly go on without her?'

'It can't, but she'll be under considerable pressure from the police not to go back on her story. I can't see Inspector Dormer giving up without a fight.'

'But if she now admits it's not true that I raped her, it'd be

47

monstrous for the police to try and force her to stand by the lies she told them.'

'She hasn't admitted telling them lies in so many words,' Rosa said carefully. 'She was a bit equivocal. Nevertheless she was obviously very upset about your being held in custody.'

'I should bloody well hope so!' Toby exclaimed heatedly. 'Couldn't you have gone round and got her to swear a statement on oath?'

'And be accused by Dormer of trying to pervert the course of justice by interfering with his chief witness?' She observed his crestfallen expression. 'I was in a very tricky position, Toby. What we must hope is that she has spoken to the police, told them what she told me and has resisted all their blandishments and threats. In which event, they'll have no alternative but to throw in their hand. They'll probably get one of their lawyers to stand up and say that the complainant is no longer available to testify and that, without her evidence, there is no case against you. At least, that's the way I'm hoping it'll go.'

'Can't you call the police and find out whether she *has* spoken to them?'

'Not without disclosing my own knowledge. That moment may arrive, but it hasn't yet.' Noticing his faintly rebellious look, she went on quickly, 'But I'm confident we shall be able to get you bail, even if the case isn't concluded next time.'

Toby was thoughtful for a while. 'Well, I suppose that's better than nothing.'

'It's a good deal better than you were expecting before I came,' Rosa remarked drily.

'That's true,' he said, flashing her one of his engaging smiles.

'Needless to say, I shall try and find out what's happened, but it's possible we'll have to wait until we get to court.' She glanced down at the notebook that lay open in front of her. 'I've also seen your cousin, Peter Rossington,' she said, fixing Toby with a speculative look.

'How's old Peter? Still a bit jumpy?'

'He did strike me as being rather unsettled.'

'I hope he didn't throw anything at you?'

Rosa shook her head. 'Not even words. Or very few.'

'How did he react when you told him what had happened to me?'

'He made some faintly disparaging remarks about you, but I couldn't tell how he really felt. As I mentioned just now, he said very little. Moreover, he made an abrupt departure when I started to press him.'

'That sounds like Peter. He's always been a bit odd, but even odder since Tricia threw him over.'

'He still seems to be infatuated with her.'

'The poor sod!'

Shortly afterwards, Rosa made to leave.

'Can't you stay longer?' Toby asked.

'I'd better go.'

'Why?'

'Because ... because I have work to do. I'll see you at court.'

'Not before then?'

'It's only three days away.'

'Don't forget our night out when this is all over!'

Rosa stood up and pushed back her hair. 'I've not forgotten,' she said.

Then with a little wave she turned abruptly and was gone.

CHAPTER 7

Three days later, however, Rosa still had no idea of police intentions.

There had been no further calls from Tricia, though this was scarcely surprising and, as far as Inspector Dormer was concerned, she reckoned that the sun, the moon and the stars would all have to change course before he vouchsafed her any information.

She arrived at court early on the morning of the remand hearing and immediately espied D.C. Fox talking to a uniformed constable on the further side of the lobby. She made a bee-line in his direction.

'What's the position today, Mr Fox?' she enquired keenly.

He glanced at her with alarm. 'Mr Gilman from the Solicitors' Branch is here to represent the police,' he said defensively. 'I believe he wants to have a word with you.'

'Does that mean you're dropping the charge?' Rosa said a bit too eagerly, for she realised at once from Fox's expression that she had spoken incautiously. But what other explanation could there be for Geoffrey Gilman's attendance? He was one of the Yard's most experienced legal operators, who normally appeared only in cases where trouble was expected and which required skilled handling.

'Mr Gilman will put you in the picture, Miss Epton,' Fox said, edging away from her.

'Is he here yet?'

'He's over at the police station talking to Inspector Dormer.'

'Well, if he wants to talk to me, I'd better go and find him,' Rosa said briskly, trying to conceal her feeling of unease at the unexpected news.

As she entered the police station, Gilman emerged through a door at the rear of the general office.

'Ah! There you are, Miss Epton,' he exclaimed with a friendly smile. 'You're the very person I wanted to see.'

'So I gathered from D.C. Fox.'

'He's told you the form, has he?'

'He's told me nothing. I'm still agog to know what's brought *you* to court on this case. I don't suppose you've come merely to ask for a further remand,' she added wryly, throwing him an enquiring look.

'No, indeed. Let's find somewhere quiet and I'll tell you what the position is. There's a room on the first floor of the court-house we can use.'

As they crossed the road together, Rosa said, 'Inspector Dormer will have you shot at dawn if he sees you treating with the enemy.'

Gilman laughed. 'He's an abrasive fellow, isn't he? He didn't actually tell me how to do my job, but I thought any moment he was going to.' He flung open a door and stood aside for Rosa to enter. Following her in, he went straight across and closed the window. 'You don't mind, do you? It's freezing in here, so let's make it short.'

He's going to put on the casual act, thought Rosa, but it'll nevertheless be a carefully calculated performance.

'I gather the police have been having a spot of difficulty with the complainant in our case,' he said lightly. 'She sounds a neurotic sort of girl and she's been leading them a bit of a dance, so we thought it might ease the situation if we called her today and took her deposition. It seems she's been worried about giving evidence and we decided it would be best for her to get the ordeal over as soon as possible, then she can relax until the trial comes up.' He gave Rosa the sort of smile that indicated they were professional equals and understood one another. 'After she's given her evidence, I'll be asking for a further remand.'

'Not in custody, I trust?'

'Good lord, no! I gather the police won't oppose bail once she's given her evidence,' he said affably.

'I see,' Rosa remarked with a thoughtful expression. 'You realise I shall want to cross-examine the witness?'

'That's your right, Miss Epton,' he replied smoothly. 'Shall we go down before we freeze to death?' At the bottom of the stairs they parted company and he said, 'See you in court shortly.'

So that's it! Rosa reflected. Obviously Tricia has had her arm twisted and Dormer's hoping to tie her down quickly before she has another change of mind. He would have been quite unscrupulous about putting pressure on her. Indeed, he may well have struck a squalid bargain with her. 'You be a good girl and give your evidence nicely and we won't oppose bail for Nash.' But the very fact that they were proposing to call her like this showed how unsure they felt about her testimony. Provided Tricia had not undergone a radical change of view since they had talked on the telephone, Rosa reckoned she was going to have an easier time with the witness than Geoffrey Gilman, who would require all his powers of persuasion and cajolery to adduce her evidence. Evidence, moreover, which must either be perjured or must oblige Gilman to drop the case there and then.

She decided it was time to find out whether Toby had arrived from prison. It was more than ever vital she should have a word with him before the court sat.

His face lit up when his cell door was unlocked and she entered.

'You look smart enough to pass for president of the bank,' she said, giving him an approving look.

He grinned. 'I suppose I did look a bit like a rapist in that other gear.' His expression became suddenly serious and he said, 'What's happening, Rosa? What have you been able to find out?'

By the time she finished telling him, he remarked, 'Sounds better all the time!'

'Now, I want you to listen to me carefully, Toby,' she said. 'I've no idea what Tricia's going to say or how she'll react once she's in the witness box, but whatever she says or does, I want you to sit tight and say nothing. No hostile looks, no muttered interventions, no interruptions of any sort. Understand?'

'I promise to be as good as Mary's little lamb.' He hesitated a moment, then said, 'There is one matter we've not talked about. Money. I want you to know that I do have a bit tucked away and there's no question of your not being paid.'

'Don't worry about that now. We'll discuss it later. Should the case go any further, the court will probably grant you legal aid.' Observing his dismayed expression, she added, 'I said *should*. I hope the question won't arise.'

'What do you think really lies behind Tricia giving evidence today?'

'I'm sure they're hoping that once she's in the box, Gilman will be able to wheedle her original story out of her: she'll be too frightened to retract what she told the police. And I've no doubt that Inspector Dormer has exploited this angle to the utmost.'

'He's virtually forcing her to commit perjury,' Toby said indignantly.

'Leave it to me to play it by ear,' Rosa replied in a mollifying tone.

Toby stood up and twisted his neck around. 'This collar's tight,' he said with a grimace. 'It's all that starchy prison food.'

'Keep your fingers crossed that you've had your last meal there. Meanwhile, don't forget what I've told you!'

'No, miss,' he said with a grin.

Rosa found the court-room considerably more crowded than on her previous visit. The clerk gave her a fleeting glance as she bowed to the magistrates and sat down, but he forebore to show any sign of recognition.

It became apparent that various minor cases were being disposed of first, before that of R. v. Nash claimed the spotlight. By the time it was called on, the court had emptied again. Rosa felt relieved, welcoming a calmer and less tense atmosphere for what lay ahead. Crowds created tension and distraction. She imagined that Gilman was even more relieved than herself, for he was going to have the brunt of examining a nervous witness on a difficult matter.

She noticed D.I. Dormer come into court and go and sit next to the uniformed court inspector. His expression was as amiable as that of a suspicious rhinoceros.

Shortly afterwards, the case was called and Toby was ushered into the dock.

When Geoffrey Gilman rose to address the magistrates, it was in the manner of a host welcoming his guests of honour.

'For reasons with which I need not trouble you,' he said with a small deprecating gesture, 'the prosecution are proposing to call their chief witness in this case today. After she has completed her evidence, I shall seek a further remand in order that the police may complete their enquiries. As you will appreciate, the offence was committed only a week ago and they still have a number of outstanding matters requiring their attention. I have already informed Miss Epton of my intention and she fully understands the position.'

All I understand, Rosa thought to herself, is that you're being excessively smooth and devious. Moreover, it had now dawned on her that there was an additional cogent reason for the prosecution adopting the course it had. Should Tricia let them down completely so that Gilman was obliged to throw in the towel, the police would be able to defend themselves against any subsequent accusation of keeping Toby in custody after their chief witness had told them she wanted to retract her statement. Now, if the worst occurred, they could reply that the matter had been resolved in court at the first opportunity. In effect, while still preparing to attack, they had built a bomb-proof shelter in which to take refuge if need arose. Rosa acknowledged someone's guile; almost certainly Geoffrey Gilman's, she felt. Dormer not only lacked the subtlety of mind, but would have been blind to possible criticism. And if not blind, certainly uncaring.

'Should you at the end of the prosecution's evidence decide that the accused has a case to answer,' Gilman continued, 'then I shall invite you to commit him for trial at the Central Criminal Court. But that stage won't be reached today.'

54

Or ever, if I can help it, Rosa reflected.

'I now call Miss Patricia Langley,' Gilman concluded, glancing toward the door through which the witness would come.

Inspector Dormer also looked in the same direction. Was it Rosa's imagination or did she detect a touch of anxiety in his expression?

Tricia came in accompanied by a woman police officer in uniform.

'Is the witness under guard?' Rosa murmured to Gilman.

'The policewoman's only there as comforter and friend,' Gilman murmured back.

'I wasn't aware that a witness was entitled to either when giving evidence,' Rosa said firmly.

Gilman assumed a martyred expression. 'Very well, don't let's argue about it!' Turning to the woman p.c., he said, 'It might be better if you stood well away from the witness box, officer.' He glanced down at Rosa. 'That make you happier?'

'Much.'

It was apparent from D.I. Dormer's expression, however, that he didn't share her satisfaction.

The witness box at Petersham Magistrates' Court resembled a miniature bandstand of the sort found in seaside towns in the twenties. It was reached by four steps and could have accommodated more than one witness at a time. Exhorted by the usher, Tricia approached the front edge of the box and took the oath in a halting whisper.

She was wrapped in a camel hair coat and stared directly ahead of her. At least, Rosa assumed that from the way she was facing, but as she had on a pair of impregnable dark glasses, her eyes could have been revolving like catherine wheels for all anyone could tell.

'Will you try and speak up, Miss Langley,' Gilman said as he rose to begin his examination-in-chief.

A slight movement of her head was the only indication that she had heard him.

'Is your name Patricia Langley?'

'Yes.'

55

'And do you live at Flat 4, 52 Fillery Street, S.W.6?'

'Yes.'

'I can't hear a word she's saying,' one of the magistrates said in a forlorn voice.

'So far she has said "yes" twice,' Gilman remarked drily. 'Miss Langley, we all realise this is an ordeal for you, but it is most important that everyone can hear your answers. Now you will try and speak up, won't you?'

This time she nodded.

'Did you attend a party on New Year's Eve?'

'Yes.'

'Was it a private party at somebody's house?'

'Yes.'

'Whose house?'

'People called Carver.'

'Did you go alone?'

'No, I took Toby Nash.'

'Do you see him in court?'

'Yes.'

'You say that you took him. Do you mean he took you?'

'No. I invited him.'

'I see. And how did you get on together at the party?'

'All right.'

'What do you mean by "all right"?'

Rosa sprang to her feet. 'Surely all right means all right,' she said.

Gilman sighed and decided to try a fresh tack.

'How long have you known Toby Nash?'

'About a year.'

'Are you close friends?'

'No.'

'Nevertheless you invited him to this party?'

'Yes.'

'And what was your relationship while you were there?'

Rosa was on her feet again.

'Haven't you already asked that question and received the answer "all right"?'

Gilman frowned. 'I must ask Miss Epton to restrict her interruptions,' he said in a lofty tone.

'I only interrupt when you stray from the straight and narrow path of permissible questions,' Rosa retorted.

Gilman turned back to the witness. 'What time did you leave the party, Miss Langley?'

'I've no idea. I didn't look at my watch.'

'With whom did you leave?'

'With Toby Nash.'

'In his car?'

'Yes.'

Gilman glanced at Tricia's statement to the police which he held in his hand. What was exercising his mind was whether he should seek the court's permission to treat the witness as hostile. If the magistrates agreed, he could then put the statement to her line by line. He knew it was what Dormer wanted.

When they had discussed the case, the D.I. had said in his most militant tone, 'If she won't come up to proof, you'll have to treat her as hostile.'

'But no jury is ever going to convict of rape where the complainant has to be treated as a hostile witness by the prosecution,' he had protested.

'No witness in one of my cases gets away with backsliding without having their tail twisted. And twisted hard,' Dormer had replied belligerently.

Recollection of this interchange came back to him as he now stood facing an obviously reluctant witness.

'So you left the party with Toby Nash in his car,' he recapitulated. 'Where did you go?'

'I don't know.'

'But you must know, Miss Langley.'

'I don't.'

'Did he drive you straight home?'

'No.'

'Miss Langley, we know you arrived at Petersham Police Station just before three o'clock in the morning of New Year's

57

Day. What were you doing between leaving the party and arriving there?'

Tricia seemed to sway slightly and she clutched the wooden rail in front of her.

'Are you all right, Miss Langley? Do you wish to sit down?'

Even as Gilman spoke, the woman police officer had sprung into action and placed a chair behind Tricia. Meanwhile, the magistrates and their clerk looked on impassively, well used to fainting witnesses.

Tricia gently subsided on to the chair and the policewoman bent over her solicitously.

'We'll adjourn for a few minutes,' the chairman announced and left the bench with his fellow magistrates.

Inspector Dormer went over to the witness box and began whispering to Tricia, so that Rosa was reminded of a boxer in his corner surrounded by anxious seconds. She decided to go and have a word with Toby who was sitting in the dock intently observing the scene.

'Surely she can't wriggle out of it by putting on a fainting act?' he said savagely. 'She was just about to cave in. Anyone could see she was skirting all round the truth. That bastard Dormer's obviously scared the daylights out of her. Can't you stop him talking to her now?'

'Keep calm,' Rosa said. 'Everything's going all right.'

'You were terrific,' Toby said in an admiring tone.

'I haven't done anything yet.'

'I mean the way you stood up to the prosecuting solicitor when he asked those improper questions.'

'Well, of course I did. It was my job to do so.'

'I know, but even so ... '

'Just because he's a man and bigger and stronger than me doesn't mean I run away from him in court.' She gave Toby a mischievous smile. 'We're both of us lawyers, ready to get away with any tricks we can.' Glancing toward the witness box, she said, 'It looks as if Tricia has been revived. I'd better return to my place.'

Shortly afterwards, the magistrates returned to court and Gilman rose to his feet.

'I gather the witness is not feeling at all well and isn't able to continue her evidence,' he said. 'In those circumstances, I must ask for the case to be remanded. I much regret not being able to go on, but there appears to be no alternative to adjourning now.'

Rosa felt as if she had been pipped at the post. She knew she had no valid objection to the proposed course. On the other hand she was sure that it would not have needed more than a few questions to topple the case altogether. It was obvious the police wanted a postponement, as time was their only hope.

'Anything you wish to say, Miss Epton?' the chairman enquired.

'If you please, there are two matters. First, as Miss Langley is part way through her evidence, it would, in my view, be most improper for any police officer to talk to her between now and the remand date. In effect, she ought to remain incommunicado so far as this case is concerned. I am sure such a direction would come well from the court.'

The magistrates blinked at her in surprise before turning to their clerk for advice. After a murmured consultation, the chairman said, 'We have no authority to give such a direction, Miss Epton, but I'm sure the police can be relied upon not to do anything improper.'

Rosa couldn't help observing Dormer's look of grim satisfaction.

'I think you said you had two matters, Miss Epton,' the chairman went on. 'What is the second?'

'I apply for bail on behalf of my client. Last week you were good enough to express a readiness to reconsider the question on his next appearance. He can offer sureties and give any undertakings you require. In particular, he will undertake not to have any contact whatsoever with Miss Langley.

'In view of this morning's turn of events, which might aptly be described as bizarre, it would, in my submission, be manifestly unfair not to grant him bail.' Rosa paused and then decided she might as well stir up a hornets' nest. 'It must surely have been obvious to everybody in court that Miss Langley was an extremely reluctant witness.'

59

'Really!' Gilman exclaimed sharply. 'I can't accept that and it's certainly not the time for making comments of that nature. Most improper of you, Miss Epton!'

The magistrates, as was their wont during forensic flurries, looked nonplussed; their clerk nodded his agreement with Gilman; and Inspector Dormer glared furiously at Rosa who remained unabashed.

'At all events,' she went on, 'I do urge you most strongly to grant my client bail.'

'Is there any police objection to bail?' the clerk asked languidly.

Gilman glanced at D.I. Dormer who rose from his seat and moved ponderously toward the witness box.

'Subject to satisfactory sureties, I don't oppose bail, your worships,' he said in a grudging tone, 'though I suggest that the accused also be required to surrender his passport. And I take note of the undertaking given on his behalf by his solicitor. Namely, that he will make no attempt to communicate in any way whatsoever with Miss Langley.' He flashed Rosa a look which told her (if further telling were needed) that he was only waiting for her to step an inch out of line before pouncing.

Indeed, as the court broke up, she overheard him say to Gilman that he intended investigating the possibility of Tricia having been nobbled.

'I'm pretty sure she has been, Mr Gilman, and no court can stop me making such enquiries as I see fit,' he had said, as Rosa walked past.

It was an hour or so before Toby's bail formalities had been completed and she waited in order to be able to drive him into town.

'You were really terrific, Rosa,' he exclaimed enthusiastically as they got into her car. 'And now I'm feeling terrific.'

'It's not all over yet,' she replied.

She had a disquieting feeling that, though a minor battle might have been won, the war itself was only about to begin.

But, with Toby in a mood of euphoria, there was no point in burdening him with any of her presentiments.

CHAPTER 8

Tricia was still feeling emotionally wrung out by the time she reached home. It had been a ghastly morning and her only thought was to go and lie down on her bed with a stiff drink at her side.

She had just mounted the steps which led to the front door, when a voice called out.

'Hello there, Tricia.'

She turned her head to find Norman Oliver just behind her, having apparently popped up from nowhere.

'Oh, hello,' she said coldly and quickly turned her back on him while she inserted her key in the lock.

'Don't usually see you about at this hour of the day,' he remarked. 'Having another day off from work, eh?'

'I had some private business to attend to,' she replied in an even chillier tone.

'You look a bit washed out. Feeling all right, are you? Like me to come up with you and make you a cup of tea or coffee?'

'No thank you.'

'It wouldn't be any trouble and I could check that bathroom heater at the same time.'

'I said, no thank you.'

'As a matter of fact, I'd like your advice, Tricia.'

'What about?' she asked without enthusiasm.

'I've always thought of you as having excellent taste,' he went on, with a smile that revealed all his nicotine-stained teeth. 'I'm going to buy some new curtains for my bedroom and I'd like your advice on the colour. If you can spare a moment ... '

'Not now, I'm afraid.'

'It won't take long.'

'I've got some urgent phone calls to make.'

'Come down to my flat when you've made them.'

61

'Tomorrow perhaps.'

'Is that a promise?' he asked eagerly.

'I'll bring down Sara or Janice. Two opinions will be better than one.' Not to mention safety in numbers, she reflected.

'It's your opinion I want,' he said with a wolfish gleam. 'Come down tomorrow evening for coffee and a liqueur. I've got lots of those miniature bottles. You can have your pick. What's your favourite?'

Tricia shook her head impatiently. 'I simply must go,' she said and shot into the house.

He really was becoming more of a pest than ever. God forbid that he should ever find out about the rape affair. He was the sort of person who would interpret it as an invitation to try something of the same sort himself.

After double-locking the flat door behind her, she went and poured herself a large brandy, which she drank standing up. She enjoyed the sensation of it coursing through her body, giving her strength and fortifying anew her determination not to go through with the case. It was that hateful man, Dormer, who had bent her will with his mixture of cajolery and hidden threats. Well, damn the threats! And damn Toby, too, for that matter! There were still moments when she wanted to lash out at him.

She put her glass down on the table and decided to go and rest on her bed for a time. The past week had been a continuous nightmare with its broken routine and the various deceptions she had been forced into to explain her absence from work.

Joyce Wyngard, as might have been expected, had been extremely inquisitive and clearly suspected that Tricia was covering something up. But Joyce had better watch out or she might find her own dark secret being revealed! Tricia had already dropped one warning hint and it seemed as if a further stronger one might be needed.

When the telephone suddenly rang, she stared at it for several seconds as she tried to decide whether to answer it. The flat was usually deserted at this hour of the day, so there wouldn't normally be anybody around to lift the receiver. Possibly, however, it was somebody who knew her movements that day.

If it was, she couldn't believe it was anybody she wished to talk to. In the end, sheer habit prevailed and she answered it.

'Is that you, Tricia?' a voice said.

'Who is that?'

'Oh, God, you can't have forgotten my voice. It's Peter. Peter Rossington.'

'Oh!'

'I thought I'd call you.'

'Oh!'

'Is it a bad time to talk?'

'What do you want to talk about?' she asked suspiciously.

'I wanted to say how upset I was to hear what had happened.'

'Happened?' she echoed coolly.

'What Toby did to you.'

'Who told you about that?'

'His solicitor. She asked to see me. If I'd known what it was all about, I'd never have gone to her office. I was terribly, terribly shocked and upset, Tricia.'

'Is that all?'

'What do you mean?'

'Is that the only reason you've called me?'

'I wondered if we mightn't see each other again?'

'Later on, perhaps. Not now.'

'I'm still crazy about you. I can't get you out of my mind. I love you, Tricia.'

'Please, Peter, don't let's go through all that again!'

'But I mean it. My life is meaningless without you. I need you so much.'

'There's no question of our meeting again while you're still in this state,' she said sharply. 'It wouldn't do you any good and it would be pure hell for me.'

'That's unkind, Tricia and I'm sure you don't mean it.'

'Whether or not it's unkind, I mean every word. We're finished, Peter. Finished! If you take my advice, you'll go back and see your psychiatrist. He may be able to help you. I can't.'

'Bitch!' he yelled down the phone. 'You're still a grade one bitch. What's more, I'm really glad you were raped. You deserved it.'

Tricia had time to hear a choked sob before she dropped the receiver. Her hands were trembling badly as she poured herself another brandy.

On their drive back into London, Toby insisted that they stop and have a drink at a pub.

'After all,' he said ebulliently, 'I don't get let out of prison every day. And we can have something to eat as well. It's coming up to lunchtime.'

Rosa agreed, but quickly added that she must return to her office immediately afterwards.

'A large Scotch?' he enquired as they made their way to the bar.

'A small cider,' Rosa said firmly. 'It's all right for you, you don't have to work this afternoon.'

'Surely you needn't either. Why don't we go to a movie?'

'I can't possibly,' she said in a shocked tone. 'Work is probably piling up on my desk even as we talk.'

'Surely it can wait?'

She shook her head. 'You're not my only client, Toby.'

'You shouldn't become a slave to routine. Enjoy yourself when the opportunity presents itself.'

'One, I do enjoy myself and two, we're all slaves to routine.'

'I like to believe that I never let routine stop me grabbing a golden opportunity.'

'Are you suggesting that an afternoon at the cinema with you is a golden opportunity not to be missed?' she enquired drily.

He grinned. 'O.K., I'll let you off if you'll come out with me later this week.'

'I'd like to.'

'What about Friday evening?'

'All right.'

'We'll have dinner at a small Italian restaurant I know where the waiters spend their time exclaiming "fantastico". It's their response to everything from an order for spaghetti to being

64

handed a dripping umbrella. I'll come and pick you up at half past seven.'

'Will you go back to work tomorrow?'

Toby made a face. 'I suppose so. I'll have to find out from Sam what he told my boss.'

'What would the bank's reaction be if they knew how you'd spent the past week?'

'The vibrations of disapproval would be felt as far away as Lands End. But they can't get rid of me if I'm innocent.'

'Not even for having deceived them about your absence?'

'They might try, I suppose. But who cares? I don't and, in any event, I shan't stay there much longer. It's merely a question of choosing my own moment to depart.'

'What would you like to do most?'

'That's the difficulty, I don't really know. You don't need a keen young assistant, do you?'

'Snaith and Epton couldn't possibly afford you.'

'It'd be a sound investment.'

'As sound as buying shares in Sahara sand!'

He grinned at her. 'As a matter of fact, I wouldn't mind having a go at being a travel agent or working for an airline. Lots of cheap travel and opportunities of ... ' His voice trailed away.

'Opportunities of what?' she asked with curiosity.

'Just opportunities, period,' he said dreamily.

Starry-eyed romantic or glib opportunist, Rosa wondered. But what's it matter, I still think he's fun. I like his lack of stuffiness and I would certainly never have dreamt that I would ever feel this way about somebody who had been charged with rape. It all goes to show you can't judge things by their label. Though of course in this instance, I knew Toby before the particular label was attached. I wonder if I'd have felt the same had I not met him till afterwards. Oh for heaven's sake, Rosa, stop this introspection! You don't have to account to anyone for your taste nor apologise for it. If you like somebody, you like them warts and all. If you're put off by the warts, that's an end of the relationship.

She was still turning these thoughts over in her mind when

65

she returned to the office, after leaving Toby to go and pick up his car and drive home.

'How'd it go this morning?' Robin Snaith asked as she poked her head round his door to show that she was back. When she had finished telling him, he said, 'It sounds as if it's all over bar the shouting.'

'I hope so,' she said with a worried frown.

'You sound doubtful. What's troubling you?'

'It's Detective Inspector Dormer,' she said. 'I neither like him nor trust him. He's not merely tough; I'm sure he's vindictive, too. I believe he's going to try and prove that I nobbled his witness.'

'But you didn't, so he'll be banging his head against a wall.'

'I wouldn't trust Tricia Langley not to shop me if it was a question of saving her own skin.'

Robin pursed his lips in thought for a while. 'You don't think Dormer would actually fabricate evidence against you?'

'I don't know,' Rosa said bleakly. 'He's a fighter and, almost certainly, a dirty fighter.'

'But even if this Langley girl does tell him you tried to dissuade her from giving evidence, that's not sufficient to bring any charge against you. He'd need corroboration and there can't be any.'

'It's not the thought of being charged that worries me, because, like you, Robin, I'm sure it won't get to that stage, but it's all the unpleasantness and harassment while he's investigating the matter that concerns me.'

'We can only cope with that as it arises,' Robin said judicially. 'Even D.I. Dormer can't overstep the mark with impunity. He may be a nasty bit of work, but don't turn him into an ogre.'

Rosa smiled. 'As always, Robin, you're full of good sense and sound advice.'

'It's always easier to bring both to someone else's problems than to one's own,' he observed wryly.

Rosa turned to go, but halted in the doorway.

66

'Toby Nash has invited me out to dinner on Friday evening,' she said in a faintly defiant tone.

'Oh, yes. And?'

'I've said I'll go.'

'Why are you telling me?' he asked after an awkward pause.

'Because I wanted you to know.'

'And now I do.'

'I can't see any professional objection, can you?'

'No-o,' he said slowly. 'It's not like a doctor seducing his patient.'

'I'm glad you say that.'

'Though you could find yourself out on a tightrope,' he added.

'In what way?'

'Having a social relationship with a client charged with rape.'

'I don't see how that puts me on a tightrope.'

'Add Dormer's vendetta if he decides to conduct one.'

'I still don't see.'

'And I doubt whether the Law Society would take a very benign view.'

'There are probably lots of matters they don't take a benign view of, which still don't amount to professional misconduct.'

'This discussion is obviously not going to get us very far,' Robin said with a small smile. 'As far as I'm concerned, you have my fullest trust and you know I'm always available for advice if you want it.'

Blowing him a small kiss, Rosa turned and departed from his office.

After she had gone, Robin sighed heavily and crossed his fingers on both hands.

Detective Inspector Dormer returned to his office in a savage mood, a not uncommon state for him.

He had gone to a great deal of trouble in connection with the hearing that morning, only to be thwarted. First of all, he had had to employ all his powers of persuasion to get Tricia to court.

67

Then relying on her promise (albeit shakily given) not to let him down, he had secured the co-operation of the magistrates' clerk and, finally, the services of Geoffrey Gilman to represent the police.

And after all that the girl had gone and ditched him. No wonder he was in a savage mood, for he was back again at square one. He felt particularly incensed with Rosa, who had no right to put spokes in his wheel by her infuriating interventions and obstructive tactics. Interfering with the course of justice, that's what it was. And if she thought she could get away with it, she had better think again. She wouldn't be the first solicitor he had put in the dock on a criminal charge.

There was a knock on his door and D.C. Fox entered.

'Thought I'd let you know, sir, that Nash's sureties have been checked and he's been allowed to leave.'

Dormer grunted. 'What about his passport?'

'He said he'd bring it here this evening, sir.'

'Supposing he decides to go to Heathrow instead?'

'I'm sure he won't do that, sir.'

'Sure, are you? I hope for your sake you're right.'

'I can call the station nearest his home and ask them to send somebody round to collect it, if you think that'd be better, sir.'

'As long as you can get hold of it promptly, I don't care what you do.' In a brooding tone, he asked, 'Did Nash and his solicitor leave together?'

'Yes, sir.'

'I reckon they've hatched a neat little conspiracy to pervert the course of justice.'

'You really do think Miss Langley's been got at?'

'It's exactly what I think. She's already admitted to me that she spoke to the Epton woman on the telephone. She told me that when I went to see her a couple of days ago. I say she told me, but I had to force it out of her. The fact that she said she took the initiative in making the call doesn't impress me at all. I think Epton got in touch with her.'

'Are you proposing to investigate that angle now, sir?'

'Of course, I am.'

68

'Isn't it a bit dodgy interviewing Miss Langley again, having regard to what was said in court this morning?'

Dormer stared at his D.C. as if he were hoisting a white flag on the field of battle.

'If I have reason to believe a crime's been committed, it's my duty to investigate. I don't pussyfoot around waiting for everyone's approval before I make a move. If that girl's been nobbled, as I believe, I'm going to find out. Now.'

'I still believe, sir, that it's a case of her regretting having ever made her complaint.'

'You saw her the night she came here,' Dormer said aggressively. 'She was in a thoroughly distressed state. She'd been sexually abused and the medical evidence supported it. In my book, that was rape.'

'I agree she was distressed, sir, but it seemed to me equally consistent with ... '

'With what? A nasty attack of flatulence?' Dormer broke in scathingly.

Fox gave a feeble smile. 'I was going to say with anger, sir.'

Dormer let out another grunt. 'Anyway, nobody's going to stop me doing my duty. And my duty in this instance is to investigate possible criminal conduct on the part of Miss Oh-so-innocent-looking Rosa Epton.' He dismissed Fox with a wave. 'You'd better go and make sure you get hold of that passport.'

As he walked away from the D.I.'s office, Fox could see no end to trouble in the Nash case, which he privately considered to be a lost cause so far as the police were concerned. He was sure the prosecution was doomed and that nothing could postpone that day.

Not for the first time in recent weeks, he wondered gloomily whether his application for transfer to another division would ever come through.

CHAPTER 9

The next morning, Tricia decided to make amends by arriving early at the office. By so doing she would be able to clear any work left over from the previous day. Mr Harris, her employer, was sure to have left some letters for typing and certainly nobody would have done any filing during her absence.

She liked her work and prided herself on her efficiency. She was aware, however, that Mr Harris had not been too pleased when she had requested a day off in order to attend to private business.

'Do you need to be away the whole day?' he had asked. 'Won't just the morning or afternoon be sufficient?'

Tricia had reasoned, however, that even if she was finished with court in the morning (as, indeed, proved to be the case) she would not feel like going into the office in the afternoon (as had certainly also been the case). But Mr Harris had murmured a trifle peevishly that he supposed it couldn't be helped, but it really was rather inconvenient and she did seem to have had rather a lot of days off recently for one reason or another.

She had never yet been given the sack and her *amour propre* would be severely affronted should she be asked to seek a job elsewhere. Not that she believed there was any immediate risk of this, if only because she was very efficient and men are generally loath to have their office lives disrupted by change.

Joyce Wyngard, the cashier-cum-accountant, was always the first to arrive and it fell to her to open the office up, which she usually did soon after eight each morning.

On this particular morning, she hadn't even had time to take off her coat or remove the fleece-lined boots which made her feet look as if they belonged to a shaggy animal, before Tricia came in.

70

'Hello, you're early,' she said, making it sound more like an accusation than a greeting.

'I thought I'd try and catch up with yesterday's work.'

'There's nothing to catch up with,' Joyce said with a faintly malicious air. 'Mr Harris got in a girl from the agency. Very good she was too. Did all his letters and filed everything away most efficiently. He was very pleased with her.'

'Oh!' Tricia said, trying not to sound put out. 'But I expect there are a few left-overs I can get on with.'

'You mean you hope so,' Joyce observed complacently. 'She was a nice girl, too. Wendy Armitage. We got her to leave us her particulars so that we can get hold of her again should the need arise, which on your present form it probably will.'

Stung by the older woman's air, Tricia said, 'I have had precisely two days off. One on account of sickness and one for personal reasons.'

'And what'll be your excuse next time?' Joyce enquired unpleasantly.

'You're in an extremely disagreeable mood this morning,' Tricia said coldly.

'It's all a question of self-discipline,' Joyce went on, as if Tricia hadn't spoken.

'What is?'

'Coming to work and not taking days off every time one has some minor ailment or thinks one'll go shopping.'

'I did not go shopping,' Tricia said angrily.

'You don't find me coming and going when I feel like it. I've not had a day off on account of sickness for over five years. And last year I even forwent my summer holiday because we were so short-staffed.'

'I wonder if that really was the reason,' Tricia remarked with a small enigmatic smile.

'What do you mean?' Joyce demanded hotly.

'I thought it might be more a question of your not daring to go away in case your sins found you out. Or rather, somebody discovered them in your absence.'

The colour drained from Joyce Wyngard's face and she

71

stared at Tricia as though seeing an apparition. Eventually she said with heavy dignity, 'I have no idea what you mean.'

Tricia threw her a glance of knowing superiority before turning away and walking off to her own office, which was next to Mr Harris' at the end of the corridor.

That stopped her in her tracks, she reflected with satisfaction, though for how long remains to be seen. She's so blinded by self-esteem that she's about as introspective as a steam-roller. Next time I'll show her quite clearly who has the whip-hand.

Rosa hadn't long been in her office that same morning before her phone rang and Stephanie, their Girl Friday, announced that a Mrs Carver wished to speak to her.

For a second Rosa couldn't think who Mrs Carver was and when she remembered that it was Philippa, she was tempted to tell Stephanie to say that she was in conference with a client and could not be disturbed. But she realised there could be no putting Philippa off for long and so decided to talk to her now rather than at an even less convenient moment.

'Rosa, darling,' Philippa exclaimed as soon as the connection was made, 'you must have wondered why I've not been in touch with you before, but I've only just heard. This very morning, in fact. I was talking to a friend whose husband sits as a magistrate at Petersham and she told me. I can't think why I've not seen anything about it in the local paper.'

'Because reporting restrictions haven't been lifted which means the press can only report the name of the accused person and the charge against him.'

'Is that something new? I'm sure I read about a case in the paper only yesterday.'

'It only applies to cases which start in the magistrates' court and which will ultimately be tried in a crown court. There's no restriction when the case gets there.'

'Rosa, you really are incredibly clever knowing all these legal things. But to get back to the case – I almost said our case. After all, it almost happened in our garden – I gather it's that young man Tricia brought.'

'Yes, Toby Nash.'

'Yes, Toby Nash. I remember the name now. I must say he did look a bit like a rapist in that dreadful yellow shirt. I don't think I spoke to him the whole evening.'

'You should have done. He's rather nice.'

'I wonder where Tricia picked him up.'

'She was engaged to his cousin at one time.'

'Oh, so that's how she met him. And did he really rape her, darling? You can tell me. I won't murmur a word to a living soul.'

'I'm defending him, Philippa. You can scarcely expect me to say he's guilty,' Rosa said with a small laugh.

'No, of course not, darling. And, anyway, I'm sure he's not.'

'What makes you say that?' she asked with a sudden quickening of interest.

'Oh, I know unfortunate girls do get raped, but not girls like Tricia Langley by young men like Toby Nash. It's a ridiculous idea. Don't you agree, Rosa?'

'Yes, I do. And I may say that he denies the charge completely.'

'So he'll get off all right?'

'I think the case will probably collapse quite soon. It almost did yesterday.'

'I don't know whether it's a good advertisement for my parties or not,' Philippa said with a giggle. 'But with you defending, it does keep it among the guests.' She paused. 'I must say, Rosa, you must have made a considerable impression on Toby Nash in a very short time.'

'It was my dancing.'

'I reckon you must have displayed some nifty footwork apart from your dancing. When does the case come up again?'

'Wednesday next week.'

'I must come along.'

'I can't stop you, Philippa, but it might be better if you didn't.'

'What harm can I do by coming?'

'It might embarrass two, if not three, of your New Year's Eve guests.'

'You and Toby, do you mean?'

'Actually, I was thinking of Tricia and Toby.'

'Mmm, I suppose you could be right. It's obvious that Tricia hasn't told any of her family or I'd have heard earlier. But, if I don't come, you must promise to keep me informed.'

Rosa couldn't help smiling at Philippa's infectious eagerness.

'All right,' she said, 'I promise to let you have progress reports.'

'Not one of your dry-as-dust legal reports, darling. I want all the spicy details.'

'You may be disappointed, because if I have my way, the case is going to collapse before we reach the spicy details.'

'What a spoilsport you are, darling! I've a good mind not to tell you what I was about to say.'

'Which was?' Rosa said equably.

'About Tricia.'

'What about her?'

'She's what Adrian's father calls a cock-teaser, if you'll pardon the expression.'

'That's interesting.'

'Not to her boy-friends, it isn't. It's only frustrating.'

'It's how Toby Nash described her was what I meant.'

'She began early, too, I gather.'

'Meaning what?'

'I thought that would hook you,' Philippa said in a gleeful tone. 'There was a scandal while she was still at school, as a result of which an art teacher got the push.'

'A male art teacher, I take it?'

'From all accounts, a very male one.'

'And how old was Tricia at the time?'

'Fifteen. According to Adrian who got it from his father who got it from an uncle of Tricia's, she led the man on and then reported him for making indecent advances. That's the first recorded incident,' Philippa went on cheerfully, 'though, for all I know, she may have started even younger. Indeed, I'd be most surprised if she didn't. She was probably waving her knickers at the gardener when she was only nine or ten.'

74

'Has she been involved in any previous court cases as a result of her propensity?'

'What a delicious expression! I must try it out on Adrian. No, not that I've ever heard and I expect I would have if there had been.'

I'm sure you would have, Rosa thought.

'Well it's been fun talking to you, Philippa,' she said, 'but I'd better get on with some work.'

'All right, darling, I'll leave you in peace, but don't forget to keep in touch. After all, think how much duller your life would have been if you hadn't come to my party!'

That was true. Truer than Philippa realised.

When the telephone rang a second time within a few minutes, the three girls, who were in the middle of their evening meal, glanced from one to the other.

'It won't be for me again,' Tricia said almost belligerently, making it clear she didn't propose to get up and answer it.

An earlier and totally unexpected, as well as unwelcome, call had been from Joyce Wyngard, who said she had been thinking things over since leaving the office and suggested that they meet sometime over the weekend to clear up the unfortunate misunderstandings that had arisen between them. Tricia had coldly rejected the suggestion by saying she would be busy both Saturday and Sunday. As far as she was concerned, Joyce could use her olive branch for kindling wood.

'All right, I'll go,' Janice said, getting up and going out into the hall. 'I bet it won't be for me. It never is when I answer it.' A few seconds later, she called out, 'It's for you, Tricia.'

'Who is it?' Tricia hissed as they passed in the doorway.

'I've no idea. It's a male. That's all I can tell you.'

'Hello,' Tricia said cautiously after picking up the receiver.

'Hi, it's Toby. Is it all right to talk to you?'

'Hang on a second while I close the door.'

She noticed Janice and Sara exchange meaningful looks as she did so.

'What do you want?' she asked, returning to the phone. 'I thought you weren't supposed to get in touch with me.'

'I felt I must speak to you and say that I don't bear any ill-will. I'm sorry you had such a rotten time in court yesterday.'

'Is that all?'

'I was wondering if we mightn't meet for a drink.'

'Do you realise that if I told the police you'd been phoning me, you'd probably forfeit your bail and end up in prison again?'

'But I thought you ... you didn't want to go on with the case,' he said in a worried tone. When this was greeted by an ominous silence, he added quickly, 'I'm sorry, Tricia ... perhaps I'd better ring off.'

When she returned to the supper table, the other two stared at her in curiosity. She sat down, avoiding their gaze, and helped herself to a piece of cheese, which she crumbled messily on her plate before finally eating a morsel.

'Are you all right?' Sara asked.

'Yes, fine.'

'You don't look fine,' Janice said in a forthright manner. 'In fact, you haven't for the past ten days. Is something the matter?'

'Nothing that won't come right,' Tricia said with a wan smile.

'I knew there was something,' Janice exclaimed. 'Why don't you tell Sara and me? We might be able to help. And, anyway, just talking about it will make you feel better. Bottling things up inside you is the worst thing you can do.'

Sara nodded her agreement.

'Honestly, I'm all right. I've had a problem, but it's as good as over.'

'Do you believe her?' Janice asked Sara and went on without waiting for an answer, 'I mean, Tricia, these phone calls you've had. They obviously unsettle you. Incidentally, that last one. The voice seemed vaguely familiar. Was it anyone I know?'

'It was Toby Nash.'

'Of course! He came and picked you up on New Year's Eve, didn't he?'

On the two or three occasions Janice had met Toby, he had

76

struck her as an extremely normal young man. She wondered why on earth Tricia had needed to shut the door to talk to him.

'Are you going away this weekend?' Sara enquired.

Tricia shook her head.

'Sara and I are going down to my parents' home in Sussex for the weekend,' Janice said.

'That's all right. I don't mind being here on my own. When are you going?'

'Friday after work. We'll probably come back on Sunday evening.' With a smile she added, 'Better not let nosy Norm know you're here alone or he'll be making slavering noises outside the front door all night.'

'Don't worry, I reckon I can cope with him all right.'

'Why don't you go and see Miss Greenwood over the weekend?' Sara said. 'She always loves a visit and we have rather neglected her recently.'

'I ran an errand to the shops for her yesterday evening,' Janice said with a note of indignation.

'Yes, I know, but we've not been in for a proper gossip with her for some time.'

Amy Greenwood lived in the flat below. She was in her early sixties and blind. But like many blind people, remarkably independent and unselfpitying. Her large black cat, Jasper, and her radio were her two constant joys in life. But she had always taken an interest in the girls in the flat above and was thought to be the only tenant with whom nosy Norm minded his ps and qs.

'If I can, I'll go down and see her,' Tricia said doubtfully.

'She'll be delighted if you do,' Janice remarked. 'She was only saying last night that she hardly knew you.'

Tricia felt she was being manoeuvred into a visit she was by no means sure she would make. The prospect of conversation with an elderly blind woman whom she scarcely knew did not appeal to her in her present mood.

Sara and Janice were showing a pressing interest in her well-being which she could do without. It would be a relief when Friday evening arrived and she had the flat to herself.

77

CHAPTER 10

After pressing the bell a second time without any response, Detective Inspector Dormer stepped back on to the pavement and stared up at the front of the house. There was definitely no light coming from the top flat.

It was five o'clock on Sunday evening and darkness had fallen. When he had called Tricia on the phone on Friday morning before she left for work, she had been extremely reluctant for him to visit her and he had been obliged to point out forcefully that she would be obstructing him in the performance of his duties if she refused. In the end he did make one concession and agreed not to come until after dark.

He remounted the porch steps and again pressed the bell of Flat 4, this time keeping his finger on the button for at least fifteen seconds.

'Can I help you?' a voice behind him asked.

'I don't know. Who are you?' Dormer stared at the man without any show of favour.

'I'm Mr Oliver. I happen to be the landlord of this building,' Norman said, adopting his haughty tone.

'Then you can help me. I'm Detective Inspector Dormer. I've come to see Miss Langley, but I can't get any answer.'

'Perhaps she's gone out.'

'She was expecting me.'

Norman frowned in a puzzled fashion.

'It's true I've not heard her go out,' he said. 'In fact, I've not seen her at all over the weekend. I do hope nothing's happened to her.'

'Why do you say that?' Dormer asked sharply. 'Why *should* anything have happened to her?'

Norman's tongue ran nervously over his lips.

'I didn't say it had ... I just ... I mean ... '

78

'Do you hold a duplicate key to the flat?' Dormer broke in.
'Yes.'
'You'd better fetch it and we'll go up and make sure all is well.'
'I'll get it right away, Inspector.'
Norman turned and hurried down the basement steps to his own flat. He had, in fact, observed Dormer's arrival, having been alerted by the slam of his car door. Thereafter he had watched him covertly while he stood in the porch ringing the bell and had speculated who he might be.
When he returned with a bunch of keys, Dormer said impatiently, 'That took you long enough. What were you doing, cutting a fresh set?'
'I had something on the stove that needed attention. I didn't want to ruin my supper, even for you, Inspector.'
'Well get on and open the door!' Dormer said.
'Would it be in order to enquire why you wish to see Tricia; I mean, Miss Langley?' Norman remarked as he led the way upstairs.
'I don't see what business it is of yours.'
'I happen to be her friend, as well as her landlord.'
'It's still none of your business. Not even if you were her grandfather.'
Norman winced. 'I beg to disagree. It's very much my business when detective inspectors come on my property.'
'I get the impression, Mr Oliver,' Dormer said with an edge to his voice, 'that you don't want me to go up to Miss Langley's flat. I wonder why that would be.'
They had arrived outside the door of Flat 4 and Norman said quickly, 'Shall I open it now?'
'Get on and don't ask daft questions!'
Inserting the key, he pushed the door open and they both peered into a completely dark flat.
'She's obviously not at home,' he said. 'I don't know whether I ought to let you in without ... er ... a warrant.'
'You can stay by my side and make sure I don't nick anything,' Dormer said briskly, pushing past him and switching on the hall light.

The living-room door was open and a quick glance revealed nothing untoward.

'That's Tricia's bedroom,' Norman said nervously, pointing at a door on the other side of the hall. 'Janice and Sara share the room next to it. They go away most weekends.'

D.I. Dormer went across and flung open the nearer door, reaching for the light switch as he did so. Norman, who remained leaning against the wall by the front-door, heard him let out a grunt and saw him dive inside the room.

When he reappeared, he gave Norman a hard, suspicious stare.

'Why are you standing over there?' he asked in a faintly menacing voice.

'I'm just keeping out of your way, Inspector,' he said uncomfortably.

'Or is it because you knew what I'd find in the bedroom?' Norman felt mesmerised by the inspector's stare, but managed to shake his head. Dormer's voice seemed to come from a long way off as he went on pitilessly, 'Miss Langley's dead. She's been murdered.'

'How was she killed?' Norman asked, glancing with a shiver toward the door as if expecting to see Tricia's ghost suddenly take shape.

He and Inspector Dormer were in the sitting-room, awaiting the arrival of further police and all those persons who descend on the scene of a murder with their various pieces of equipment. Dormer had lost no time at all in phoning the local station and reporting his discovery.

'Suffocated,' he said laconically.

'What with?'

'Her pillow.' Observing Norman closely, he added, 'It looked as if she'd been sexually assaulted.'

'Poor child! What a terrible thing to have happened!'

'She was certainly an attractive girl,' Dormer said matter-of-factly.

'Sweet-natured, too.'

'Oh, yes? I wouldn't know about that.'

'Was she in trouble with the police?' Norman went on, seemingly eager to talk. 'I don't yet know why you came to see her.'

'As far as I'm concerned, it's still none of your business, though I expect you'll find out all in good time. Meanwhile, I have a number of questions to ask you, Mr Oliver. First, when did you last see her alive?'

'It must have been Friday evening when she came back from work.'

'Did you speak to her then?'

'No, I just happened to be looking out of the window when she came in.'

'What time was that?'

'Between half past five and six.'

'Did she have any visitors that evening?'

'I wouldn't know. I always go out and have a drink on Friday evening.'

'How long were you out?'

'From soon after six until about eleven o'clock. I don't mean I was drinking the whole of that time.'

'It wouldn't matter to me if you had been. I'm only interested in establishing how long you were out.'

Norman's puzzled expression suddenly gave way to one of horror.

'You don't think she was murdered on Friday evening?' he said aghast.

'That'll be for the doctor to say. But she's certainly been dead some time.'

'How awful to think she may have been lying up here dead for forty-eight hours.'

'You can count yourself lucky she was suffocated and not stabbed or you might have had blood dripping through your ceilings. Incidentally, who lives in the flat below?'

'Miss Greenwood. She's a blind lady.'

'Blind, eh?' Dormer said with interest. 'Then she'll probably have acute hearing. She'll have to be interviewed. And who lives in the ground-floor flat?'

81

'Mr and Mrs Gupta. They're a young Indian couple with a small baby. But they're away at the moment.'

'For the weekend, do you mean?'

'They've gone back to India on holiday. It's their first visit in five years.'

'All go for some!'

Dormer was about to ask a further question when they heard the chatter of voices on the stairs.

'Who'll that be?' he asked.

'It's probably Janice and Sara returning.'

'All right, you stay where you are,' Dormer said, going out into the hall and opening the front door as the two girls arrived on the landing.

'I'm Detective Inspector Dormer, not a burglar,' he said quickly. 'I'm afraid I have bad news for you. Your flat-mate, Miss Langley, has been murdered. Other police officers will be arriving here shortly, but meanwhile I'd like to ask you a few preliminary questions. Let's go into the sitting-room.'

The girls glanced warily at their landlord.

'It's all right,' Dormer said. 'He let me into the flat.' With a small grim smile, he added, 'He's not under arrest.'

It quickly transpired that Janice and Sara had not seen Tricia since Friday morning when they left for work and that they hadn't returned to the flat before going down to Sussex that evening. They had no idea what plans Tricia had for the weekend, but they related how she had recently received a number of telephone calls that had seemed to upset her.

'Do you know who from?' Dormer enquired.

'One was from a boy she knew called Toby Nash.'

Dormer's expression gave nothing away as he received this piece of information.

Finally, the two girls gave it as their joint opinion that Tricia had not been her usual self for some while. She had mentioned a personal problem, but they had no idea what it was.

When they finished speaking, they turned and stared in a speculative sort of way at their landlord who shifted uncomfortably in his chair.

Dormer hoped that whoever turned up from the local station

82

might be somebody junior to himself. It seemed a not unreasonable hope on a Sunday evening. But clearly the officer who did attend would take charge, the crime being on his patch.

When he heard fresh and heavier footsteps on the stairs (the main house door having been left unlocked on his instructions) he walked out on to the landing to greet the new arrivals.

'Detective Inspector Dormer, is it?' asked a lithe, dark haired man younger than himself. 'I'm Detective Superintendent Savill.' He turned and gestured in the direction of the two men standing on the top stair just behind him. 'Detective Sergeants Holthouse and Speed.'

Though he had never had any official contact with Savill, Dormer knew him by sight, having had him pointed out at a Yard social function. This was shortly after Savill had received a medal for gallantry for disarming and arresting an armed robber who had shot dead a young police constable and was firing wildly at everyone in sight. He was now second-in-command of his divisional C.I.D. and resembled a competent business executive more than a senior police officer.

Savill went on, 'I'm afraid Detective Chief Superintendent Earnshaw is in hospital at the moment or he'd have come along. As you probably know, he makes a point of personally attending the scene of every murder on the division. He's even been known to dash from one to the next.'

Dormer acknowledged all these introductory remarks with a series of non-committal grunts. Then turning, he led the way into the flat.

'I've got the landlord and the deceased's two flat-mates in there,' he said, indicating the sitting-room with a wave of his hand and moving toward Tricia's bedroom door. 'The deceased is just as I found her about half an hour ago.'

He stood aside to let Savill go in first and watched him glance all round the room before focusing his attention on the body which lay on the bed, with the pillow still over her face. Savill lifted it almost daintily and gazed at Tricia's discoloured and congested features. Then he gently touched her forehead as if she might only be asleep and he didn't wish to wake her up.

83

'How long would you say she's been dead?' he asked, turning to Dormer.

'I'd say anything between thirty-six and forty-eight hours. You'll note that rigor mortis has worn off.'

Savill nodded thoughtfully and let his gaze travel down her body.

She was lying on her back on top of the bed and was fully dressed, except for the fact that her skirt was pulled up above her waist and a pair of ripped panties lay beside her left hand. The whole of her lower abdomen was exposed.

'Not much doubt what the motive was,' Savill observed.

'Unless somebody wanted us to think it was a sexual assault when really the motive was quite different.'

'Which obviously brings us to why you're here, Inspector,' Savill said, fixing Dormer with a quizzical look. When Dormer had finished explaining, Savill said, 'That certainly gives the case a different complexion. It'll obviously be of assistance if you can stay with the investigation. Would you mind if I arranged that with our respective guvnors?'

'I'd be glad. I feel I've been cheated by this girl's death and people who cheat me usually end up regretting it.'

Savill gave him a curious look, but said nothing. He had heard about Dormer's reputation as a tough, abrasive officer and hoped he had not erred in making his proposal. In theory, it was obvious and commonsensical and he could now only trust it would work out that way in practice. But Dormer's tone had carried a note of vindictiveness which he hadn't cared for. He ran a hand over his springy black hair and sighed.

'Once the doctor and the forensic people have been, we can really get down to work. I'm not sure that I oughtn't to accompany you, Inspector, when you go to see this chap, Nash. He sounds like a prime suspect.'

'I think I'm more likely to get something out of him on my own. I'd like to catch him by surprise tonight and you're going to be caught up here for the next few hours.'

'O.K., but keep me in touch.'

'Will do.'

'I take it we can accept what the two girls have told you without question?'

'It's my rule never to accept anything without question,' Dormer retorted bluntly.

Savill swallowed the comment that sprang to his mind and which he couldn't politely make in the presence of two sergeants. For that matter, it couldn't be made politely at all. It also suddenly dawned on him that Dormer had so far avoided calling him 'sir' on a single occasion. It didn't worry him, save to add to his doubts about the wisdom of enlisting the D.I.'s co-operation in the investigation. Ah well, he could always send him packing back to his own division if things didn't work out.

'What about Mr Oliver, the landlord?' he asked. 'Ought we to regard him as a suspect?'

'In my view, yes. He's a nasty bit of work. Typical sex molester.'

Savill turned to one of the sergeants. 'Check out his name with C.R.O., Peter. If we find he has any previous for sex offences, it'll upgrade him as a suspect.' Turning to the other sergeant, he said, 'Go and visit the blind lady in the flat below, Brian, and find out if she heard any strange noises coming from up here over the weekend. Meanwhile, Peter, you can accompany Mr Oliver back to his own flat and get a statement from him.' Glancing at Dormer, he said, 'I can see that you're raring to go and interview Nash, Inspector. Don't let me keep you!'

CHAPTER 11

Patience had never been Dormer's long suit, but there were some occasions when he was prepared to exhibit an almost inexhaustible supply of that virtue. One was when he had the scent of prey in his nostrils.

Accordingly, when he arrived at the block of flats in Swiss Cottage where Toby lived, but found nobody at home, he was content to sit in his car and wait. He had parked across the street from where he could observe all comings and goings. Before settling down to do so, however, he entered a nearby public telephone kiosk and dialled Toby's number to satisfy himself there really wasn't anybody at home and it wasn't a question of the doorbell being out of action.

Reassured on this point he returned to his car, switched on the radio and sat back. The fact that he had no home life in the normal sense meant that he didn't feel the call of his own hearth on a Sunday evening. Or on any other evening, for that matter.

His wife had walked out on him fifteen years ago and was now married to a publican in the Birmingham area. There were weeks on end when he forgot that he ever had been married. A widowed sister kept house for him. It was an arrangement that suited both of them and had nothing to do with sentiment or family ties. As a neighbour had remarked, the only bond they appeared to have in common was ungraciousness. They lived their separate lives beneath the same roof with a minimum of communication.

Like a denizen of the jungle lying in wait for its prey, he sat in the car awaiting Toby's return.

Shortly before half past ten he saw him come round a street corner, accompanied by another young man. His gait appeared unsteady and it was obvious where he had been spending the evening.

When they were about twenty yards from the entrance to the flats, he got out and walked across the street.

'Good evening, Mr Nash,' he said, with a mocking emphasis on the word mister.

Toby peered at him. 'Oh God, it's you!' he exclaimed. Turning to his companion he went on, 'He's that policeman, Sam. The one I've told you about.' He was swaying slightly and reverted his attention to Inspector Dormer. 'What are you doing here?'

'I want to talk to you.'

'You can't ... You've no right ... I want my solicitor.'

'I suggest we go across and sit in my car.'

'Not bloody likely!'

'If you're not careful, I'll arrest you,' Dormer said fiercely.

'You can't arrest me. I've not done anything.'

'You've broken the terms of your bail. I'd be fully justified in taking you into custody.'

Toby's mouth sagged open. 'Wha d'you mean?'

'You got in touch with Miss Langley in breach of your undertaking. That's grounds for my taking you back into custody, so if you're sensible you'll come and sit in my car so that I can talk to you.'

'Why should I?' Toby asked stubbornly.

'Because it's the softest option you have.'

'I want my friend to come, too.'

Dormer shook his head. 'Just you and me.'

'You'd better do as he wants, Toby,' Sam broke in. 'I'll go up and phone Rosa.'

Toby nodded vigorously. Then with a puzzled frown, he turned back to Dormer and said, 'I think you're bluffing. If you'd wanted to arrest me, you'd have done so.'

'Don't put me to the test!' Dormer muttered in a harsh voice. 'Now come over to my car before I adopt less friendly methods.'

'Did you hear that, Sam? He threatened me. Anyway, since

87

when have you ever been friendly, Detective Inspector Dormer?'

The next thing he knew, he had been hustled across the street and thrust into the back of the car.

'I'll report you for assault,' he said furiously. 'You've wrenched my arm.'

'Rubbish. If I hadn't helped you across, you'd have been knocked down by a car. Now, let's get down to business ... '

'You're squashing me,' Toby protested, trying to push the other man away from him.

'I'll do worse than squash you, if you don't shut up. When did you last see Miss Langley?'

'In court.'

'I don't believe you.'

'It's true.'

'What about your phone call to her?'

'What phone call?'

'The phone call that could land you back in Brixton.'

'I want my solicitor.'

'Where were you on Friday evening?'

'Out.'

'Where?'

'Having dinner with a friend.'

'Fixing up your alibi, were you?'

'I don't know what you mean.'

'Who was the friend?'

'I don't want to say.'

'My belief is that you visited Miss Langley's flat that evening.'

'I haven't been near her flat since ... since New Year's Eve when I picked her up to go to the party.'

'Admit you visited her last Friday evening.'

'I tell you I didn't.'

'Did you go there on Saturday?'

'No! Why don't you ask her if you don't believe me?'

Dormer shot him a thoughtful glance. 'You had an excellent reason for visiting her, didn't you?'

'No.'

'Of course you did. You wanted to dissuade her from giving further evidence against you.'

'She'd already made it plain in court that she was a reluctant witness.'

'As a result of your earlier pressure.'

'No. It was her own decision.'

'My belief is that you and your solicitor put pressure on her to retract her allegation.'

'We did no such thing.'

'I'll find out soon enough if you did. Don't think you're in the clear yet, because you're not by a long way.'

'Why don't you ask Tricia herself?' Toby demanded in a tone close to hysteria. 'She'll tell you it isn't true.'

'Come off it, *Mr* Nash. You know quite well I can't ask her. That's something you made sure of, isn't it?'

'I don't understand.'

'Because she's dead,' Dormer said brutally. 'As if you didn't know!'

'Tricia dead? I don't believe it. You're bluffing again.'

'She was murdered by someone and I suspect that someone was you.'

'I don't believe it,' Toby said, shaking his head in bewilderment.

'My theory is that when she refused to yield to your pressure not to give further evidence, you killed her.'

'No!' Toby shouted. Then in a quieter voice, he asked, 'When did you discover her body?'

'This evening. I imagine you've been wondering the whole weekend when it would be found.'

Toby looked at his inquisitor with hatred. 'You enjoy twisting everything I say, don't you?'

'You watch your tongue,' Dormer retorted angrily. 'I don't appreciate that sort of thing coming from a young man who's committed rape, conspiracy to pervert the course of justice and murder all in the space of two weeks.'

'You're trying to frighten me,' Toby said, swallowing hard.

'I don't frighten people. They frighten themselves by what

89

they've done. By the way, perhaps you'd now like to tell me who you were having dinner with on Friday evening?'

'It was Miss Epton,' Toby said stiffly.

Dormer gave a nod. 'I somehow thought it might be. Very convenient. Very convenient, indeed!' After a pause, he added, 'I'll be in touch with you again shortly, *Mr* Nash. You've not seen the last of me by a long chalk.'

He watched Toby cross the road and enter the block where he lived. He resembled someone trudging up a beach after an exhausting swim. Then in a series of slow, deliberate moves, Dormer started his car and moved away from the kerbside.

He was moderately satisfied with the outcome of the interrogation. It had had the effect of putting the wind up young Master Nash and that was all to the good. On the other hand, the walls of a police station provided the most persuasive atmosphere for that sort of interview. But without alerting the local police, which he hadn't wanted to do, his car had afforded the best alternative.

As he stopped at traffic lights, a small Honda turned across his front and he recognised Rosa at the wheel.

He noted her anxious expression. Before long he would be interrogating her, too. It was frustrating that he couldn't just haul her along to the station for questioning. Instead he would have to make an appointment and probably see her at her own office. Lawyers carried a certain amount of clout and were all too ready to raise hell if they found themselves treated in the same manner as many of their clients.

Moreover, he knew that Rosa would fight him all the way, which made him look forward with even greater relish to her ultimate downfall.

Sam opened the door to Rosa when she arrived. It was her first visit to the flat and she had found herself walking down the corridor in the wrong direction on getting out of the lift. All the doors looked exactly alike and, moreover, were capriciously numbered.

'I'm so glad you're here,' he said. 'I'm afraid it's worse than I told you.'

'You mean, Toby's been arrested?'

'No. It's Tricia, she's been found dead in her flat. Murdered.'

'Murdered!' Rosa said incredulously. Then glancing past Sam into what appeared to be the living-room, she asked anxiously, 'Where's Toby?'

'In the bathroom, throwing up. Dormer's visitation has left him shattered.'

'That's hardly surprising, given the sort of man Detective Inspector Dormer is.'

Sam ushered her into the sitting-room and stood hovering in the doorway.

'Would you like some coffee? I'm sure Toby could do with some. We'd been out drinking and he had quite a skinful of beer. I'll go and see if he's all right.'

Left alone, Rosa gazed round the room. It contained an armchair and a sofa whose cushions clearly came from a different source. There was a bookshelf filled with well-worn paperbacks and over in one corner a record player sitting on the floor with an untidy pile of records beside it. Removing a copy of *Penthouse* magazine from one end of the sofa, Rosa sat down. She had barely done so when Toby came into the room. He gave her a wan smile and sat down beside her.

'Do I look as terrible as I feel?' he asked.

Rosa studied his green-tinged appearance. 'I think you probably do. But that's hardly surprising. Beer, followed by a dose of D.I. Dormer, is enough to upset the strongest constitution.'

'You've heard about Tricia?'

'Yes, Sam told me. But I want to hear exactly what Dormer said to you.'

Toby had just begun when Sam came back into the room bearing three mugs of coffee on a tin tray.

'I hope nobody wants it white,' he said, 'because we're out of milk. Typical of a bachelor establishment,' he added, turning to Rosa. He handed round the mugs. 'I'll leave you two to talk. I'm off to have a bath.'

'Don't lock the door,' Toby called out anxiously.

91

'It's about the one time I might,' he said over his shoulder. 'Put your head out of the kitchen window if you have to make another dash.'

For the next ten minutes Toby talked while Rosa listened. When he had finished, she said, 'He's not just a bully, he's a dishonest bully. He knew quite well he couldn't have your bail revoked. Tricia's death has put an end to the case.'

Toby looked at her unhappily. 'I'm terribly sorry I've landed you in such a mess.'

'I won't pretend I couldn't do without Inspector Dormer's attentions,' she replied. 'But beyond being time-consuming, the prospect doesn't alarm me.'

She spoke robustly entirely for Toby's benefit. In fact, she felt considerably less sanguine about the immediate future than she wished to admit.

Though she wasn't personally frightened of Dormer, she realised that he could cause her a great deal of harassment which was bound to affect Snaith and Epton. And this prospect did concern her. It was not sufficient having a clear conscience about his ridiculous allegations. The fact remained that he was intent on making as much trouble for her as he could. Indeed, she would not put it beyond him to try deliberately to frame her. He chose to believe that she and Toby had suborned his witness and he would set out to prove it by means fair or foul.

On the other hand, she thought even D.I. Dormer would think twice before trying to frame them for murder.

The fact that she and Toby had spent the supposed evening of the murder in one another's company now looked a somewhat dubious occurrence. It was certainly one she wouldn't choose to have publicised. Nor did she relish the possibility of having to admit she had spent the night with a client who had been charged with rape. This could be potentially damaging to their firm and it was Robin's reaction that was uppermost in her mind. The thought of having let him down filled her with black despair.

'I suppose Dormer will want to see *you* tomorrow,' Toby observed, breaking in on her thoughts. 'What'll you tell him?'

'That depends on what he asks me. In general, I shall defy him to prove his crazy allegations.'

He put out a hand and rested it on hers. 'I can only repeat how sorry I am to have got you into this mess,' he said in a contrite tone. 'I hope you don't regret having ever met me.'

'I'd hardly have come along this evening if that were so.'

'You might have come out of a sense of professional duty.'

'Yes,' she said thoughtfully, 'I suppose I might. And I think we ought to keep our relationship on a strictly professional footing from now on. If Dormer gets in touch with you, tell him that you refuse to see him other than in the presence of your solicitor. I'll call him tomorrow – if he doesn't call me first – and underline that message.

'I won't say you have nothing to worry about, Toby, because having somebody like Inspector Dormer around is akin to having a tiger prowling in your backyard. What we must hope is that the police solve Tricia's murder nice and quickly. Also we can be thankful that Dormer isn't in charge of the enquiry. It'll be an officer from the division in which she lived.'

Toby nodded morosely and Rosa leaned over and kissed him lightly on the lips.

'That's for remembrance,' she said.

CHAPTER 12

After the best part of an hour's talk with Janice and Sara, Detective Superintendent Savill felt that he had acquired a wealth of useful information about the dead girl. Her attitudes and habits, as well as her general nature, had taken shape in his mind as they talked. They had also provided him with a number of leads which would be worth following up.

It had interested him to note that, though both girls had been careful not to point an accusing finger in any particular direction, it clearly wouldn't surprise them if his enquiries resulted in the arrest of their landlord. They denied having any reason to suspect him of violence, but they obviously regarded him as the prototype of a sexual offender.

The other person about whom they talked, reluctantly at first but later more freely under Savill's friendly questioning, was Peter Rossington. They saw him as a decent, if slightly unstable, young man who had been very much in love with Tricia and whom she had unfeelingly cast aside.

'It's not that she lacked feeling,' Janice explained, 'but rather that she was bad at handling personal situations.'

'One gets the impression,' Savill observed, 'that her beauty outmatched her maturity.'

Sara nodded. 'That's it exactly. She knew she was attractive and was quite ready to trade on it, but then couldn't cope with the situation that developed.'

'What about Toby Nash?' Savill asked. 'Might he have murdered her?'

'Definitely not,' Janice said, while Sara nodded. 'Toby didn't have any hang-ups over Tricia.'

'I gather from your answer that Tricia never told you what happened on New Year's Eve?'

They shook their heads and looked at him expectantly.

94

'What *did* happen on New Year's Eve?' Janice asked with bursting curiosity.

When he finished telling them, Sara said, 'Well, well! That explains her recent behaviour.'

'If Toby did rape her, I bet it was because she didn't object,' Janice remarked.

'In that event, it wouldn't be rape,' Savill said. 'Absence of consent is a vital element of the offence. However, Inspector Dormer seems to believe it was a true bill and that pressure was being put on her to retract her allegation.'

'Is that why he was here this evening?'

Savill nodded. 'If Toby Nash or anybody else was attempting to defeat the course of justice, it was his duty to investigate.'

'I still can't believe that Toby raped her,' Sara said.

'I suppose I oughtn't to say this,' Janice remarked, 'but I can imagine going to bed with Toby would be a definite fun experience.'

'Janice!' Sara exclaimed in a tone that was half-shocked and half-amused.

'You're not going to write that down in your little notebook, are you?' Janice said, glancing at Savill with sudden alarm.

'As far as I'm concerned, it was an off-the-record observation,' he replied with a grin.

If he had learnt much from the girls, they, for their part, had been enchanted by him. He had been friendly and easy to talk to and they had had no idea that Detective Superintendents in real life could be so good-looking. Particularly if you went for the handsome early middle-aged type.

While they talked, there had been constant interruptions with the arrival and departure of various experts and additional officers. The police doctor had been and gone, but now the pathologist had arrived to make a preliminary examination before the body was removed to the mortuary for his more detailed attention.

'Will one of you be breaking the news to her parents?' Savill asked, getting up from his chair. Observing their horrified expressions, he went on, 'It's all right, you don't have to. We have a procedure for this sort of thing. We'll get in touch with the police at their home in Somerset and ask them to go round to the house.'

'Actually, we've never met her parents,' Sara said. 'I know they come up to London occasionally, but Tricia never asked them to the flat, nor were we ever invited to meet them at their hotel. She wasn't a friendly girl in that way. She liked to keep people she knew in separate compartments.'

Savill nodded. 'What about her employer? Somebody ought to tell him what's happened.'

'All I know is that his name's Mr Harris,' Janice said. 'And there was a Joyce somebody or other whom Tricia cordially disliked. This Joyce person had worked there for years and used to go jogging on Wimbledon Common. That's the only reason I remember her.'

At that point, Detective Sergeant Speed came into the room and asked to speak to Savill outside.

'I've interviewed Miss Greenwood, sir. She's the blind lady in the flat below. She's quite sure she heard footsteps up here on Friday evening. She's equally certain she didn't hear a sound either on Saturday or today. She didn't think anything of it as she knew the girls often went away at weekends.'

'Was she able to distinguish any of the footsteps?'

'She thinks there were two people, sir. One had a heavier tread than the other.'

'Tricia Langley and a man,' Savill said thoughtfully. 'What time was this on Friday evening?'

'She says it was sometime between seven and half past. The interesting thing, sir, is that she has the distinct impression of having heard the heavier footsteps on a previous occasion.'

'But she had no idea to whom they belong?'

'None.'

'Would the footsteps have come from the living-room?'

'Yes, sir. Hers is directly beneath.'

'And what's under Tricia's bedroom?'

'An unfurnished room she doesn't use.'

'The poor soul must have thought a herd of buffalo had got loose up here this evening.'

'She was only returning home as I went down to see her. A

96

friend picks her up in his car on Sunday evenings and drives her to church. We met on the landing outside her front door.'

'How did she take the news of Tricia's death?'

'She was shocked all right, but in a more general sort of way. She talked about London no longer being a safe city to live in. I think she'd have been more upset if it had been one of the other two. She said she knew them much better. She didn't say so in words, but I think she regarded the dead girl as a bit stand-offish compared with her two flat-mates.'

Savill absorbed this information with a thoughtful expression.

'Thanks, Brian,' he said. 'That's all useful stuff.' He turned and entered Tricia's bedroom just as Dr Bratbury, the pathologist was completing his examination. The doctor glanced up and made a grimace.

'Poor kid, whatever she'd done, she didn't deserve this,' he remarked. 'Have you got a suspect lined up yet? A boy-friend with violent tendencies?'

Savill shook his head. 'I've got a few leads, but nothing to suggest an immediate arrest. What can you tell me, doctor?'

'Not much yet, I'm afraid. At least, no more than you can deduce for yourself. She was obviously suffocated with the pillow and she's probably been dead for around forty-eight hours.' His eyes glinted behind his gold-rimmed spectacles as he added wryly, 'I got both those facts from one of your officers when I arrived.'

'Had she been sexually assaulted?'

'Can't answer that until I've made a more detailed examination and taken swabs. There's certainly some bruising on the inner thighs. It looks as if somebody tried to have intercourse with her, but I'm not yet in a position to tell you whether he succeeded.'

A few minutes later, Savill popped his head round the sitting-room door.

'They're about to take away Tricia's body, so I'd stay in here until they've gone. I'm going to seal her bedroom in case we need to go over it again. After that, we'll leave you in peace.'

97

'You wouldn't catch me going in there anyway,' Sara said, with a shiver.

'Why don't you go and stay with friends for a few nights?' Savill said.

The girls looked at each other before Janice said, 'The sooner we get used to living with what's happened the better. It'd probably be worse coming back to an empty flat in a couple of days time.'

Savill made his way downstairs and had reached the bottom before remembering that Sergeant Holthouse was presumably still interviewing the landlord (or Nosy Norm as he now thought of him since talking to the girls).

He peered down into the basement area from the porch. The front-room curtains were pulled, but he could see a shadow moving around inside. A few moments later, the door into the area opened and Sergeant Holthouse emerged. Seeing his Detective Superintendent standing at the top of the steps, he came hurrying up.

'Are you waiting for me, sir?'

'No. But I was wondering whether to come down and see how you were getting on.'

'I've taken a statement of sorts from him, sir, but I reckon it'll be only the first of many.'

'Not very forthcoming, was he?'

'He's one of those people who answers every question with a saga of antecedent history. You only realise later that it has no bearing on what you asked. But I tell you one thing, sir. He's a scared man.'

'It might be worth having him along to the station for questioning,' Savill said thoughtfully. 'If he's frightened, it'd be useful to find out why. On the other hand, I'd like to have more ammunition before tackling him. Now if we were to find out he's on record as a sex offender, we've really got something to go on. At the moment we've nothing specific.'

'Of course, sir, knowing that the dead girl was in the flat alone over the weekend gave him the opportunity of trying to make a pass at her.'

'I've not overlooked that, Peter. It also fits in with what the other two girls have told me. But I'd still like to have something specific against him before giving him a roasting. Maybe forensic will come up with something, even if CRO don't. I'm hoping that whoever it was has left behind a few tell-tale clues in the bedroom.'

Any further discussion was interrupted by Sara who came dashing out of the front door.

'Thank goodness you're still here,' she said breathlessly. 'There's just been a phone call from Tricia's ex-boyfriend, Peter Rossington. Janice is talking to him now. Can you come up?'

Taking the steps two at a time, Savill raced back upstairs. The flat door was wide open and Janice stood in the hall dangling the receiver in her hand.

'He's rung off,' she said in a forlorn voice.

'Where was he speaking from?'

'He never said. He was in a terrible state. Almost incoherent at times.'

Savill frowned. 'What was he phoning about?'

'He went on and on about not meaning what he'd said on the phone the other day. He said he'd been terribly upset about it ... and, well he just rambled on saying the same thing.'

'Did he know he was talking to you, Janice?' Savill asked.

'He must have done ... I mean, as soon as I lifted the receiver, the words started pouring out. I recognised his voice (nobody can sound quite like Peter when he's in one of his excitable moods) and I said immediately, "it's Janice, Peter".'

'Yes?'

'He just went on, so then I broke in and told him Tricia wasn't here. But God knows if he heard me or took it in, because he just went on repeating about not meaning what he'd said on the phone.'

'Have either of you any idea what he *had* said on the phone?'

They shook their heads. 'None,' Janice said. 'I suppose he spoke to Tricia some time when we weren't here.'

'You said, Janice, that you told him Tricia wasn't here. Am I to understand that you didn't tell him she was dead?'

'I thought you mightn't want me to. And, anyway, I'd have

99

been scared as to what he might do. From the sound of him, he was capable of jumping off a high building.' She bit her lip. 'I'm sorry I couldn't keep him talking until you got here, but he rang off without any warning.'

'Don't blame yourself about that. You did very well,' Savill said. 'The main thing now is to find him.'

'Do you think it could have been he who killed Tricia?' Sara asked in an anxious voice.

Savill gave a shrug. 'I've no idea until I find him. But I do know that I have a number of pressing questions that require his answer.'

CHAPTER 13

Rosa always arrived at her office by nine and sometimes earlier. On Monday she was not due in court until eleven thirty and then at one which was within walking distance. It was also Robin's invariable practice to call in at the office before going to court.

After a restless night, she arrived shortly before nine o'clock that morning and sat on edge in her room with the door open until she heard her partner come in.

'I need your advice, Robin,' she said, appearing in his doorway before he had even reached his desk. He gave her a quick, appraising look.

'Sure. Close the door and come and sit down.'

Her face had a pinched, worried expression and he felt he didn't need three guesses as to the cause. Something had happened over the weekend in connection with her rape case.

It took her twenty minutes to retail the latest developments. At the end she said, 'And now go ahead and bawl me out. It's what I deserve.'

'Even Homer may nod occasionally. Or words to that effect. But I doubt if anyone bawled him out, except possibly Mrs Homer. What we have to do is decide your stance when Inspector Dormer comes beating on the door. In the first place, I suggest I ought to be present at any interview.' Rosa nodded emphatically. 'Secondly, I suggest you admit what the police already know or what they can prove without much difficulty. It's usually the best policy where one is innocent and has nothing to hide.' He added wryly, 'But not otherwise.'

'I don't propose to tell him that Toby spent Friday night with me,' Rosa said defiantly.

'I see no reason why you should. It only becomes relevant if

101

it's suggested that Toby killed the girl at an hour when he was, in fact, in your bed. That suggestion may never be made. After all, if she was murdered in the earlier part of Friday evening, where either of you was later is irrelevant . . . '

'You know as well as I do, Robin, that if the police suspect him of murder, they'll want to discover how he spent the whole of that evening. Not just the hour either side of her death.'

'Then they may have to be told.'

Rosa gave a small shiver. 'Dormer would crucify me, if he found out.'

'It may have been indiscreet or incautious, but it wasn't a crime. In any event, from what you've told me, I have the feeling that Dormer is going to be more interested in trying to prove a conspiracy to pervert the course of justice against you than a murder charge.'

'In his mind the two offences are linked,' Rosa said. 'The one leads inevitably to the other.'

'The murder is a *fait accompli*: the attempt to pervert the course of justice is a figment of Dormer's imagination.'

'I wish to God Toby had never called Tricia the other evening,' she remarked with feeling.

'I agree, it was extremely foolish of him.'

'Dormer's sure to suggest that I put him up to it.'

'I think you must be prepared to deny it.'

'Of course I shall deny it,' she said hotly. 'I'm not so besotted with Toby Nash that I identify myself with everything he does. Come to that, I'm not *besotted* with him at all.'

Robin said nothing. In his view, Rosa was suffering from as acute an attack of client identification as he could recall. Even so, he remained confident that her considerable common sense would pull her through, if not totally unscathed, at least without lasting damage to her psyche. This time, however, their firm looked like becoming involved in a way it had not been on previous occasions and that was regrettable.

He gave her a rapid glance as she sat staring at the floor with a dejected expression. Poor Rosa! On the other hand, thank goodness she didn't get struck down too often by this capricious virus.

102

Inspector Dormer's appointment to see Rosa was for half past four that afternoon. He had telephoned in the morning not long after her discussion with Robin Snaith, declaring that he had been trying to reach her for half an hour but had been thwarted by their telephonist.

Rosa later discovered that Stephanie's blunt refusal to connect him was partly because she knew that Rosa and Robin were closeted together, but chiefly because she took exception to his manner, which she found both aggressive and rude.

'I want to see you urgently,' Dormer said. 'Is this morning convenient?'

'No, I shall be in court.'

'What about two o'clock then?'

'I'm afraid half past four is the earliest I can manage,' Rosa said coolly.

'I suppose you expect me to come to your office?'

'As it's you who wish to see me, yes.'

'I'll be along at half past four.'

'What do you want to see me about?' Rosa enquired as he was about to ring off.

'I'm surprised you need telling.'

'But I do, if you expect me to see you when you arrive.'

'I'm sure Nash has told you I saw him last night?'

'Yes.'

'Then you know why I want to talk to you,' he said testily and rang off.

Promptly at half past four he and D.C. Fox arrived at the offices of Snaith and Epton and were shown into the small, gloomy waiting-room.

After sitting there fuming for two minutes, Dormer turned to Fox.

'Go out into the corridor and make noises. I don't propose sitting here much longer.'

Fox obediently left the room. Outside he peered around anxiously until he spotted Stephanie through a half-open door sitting in front of her small switchboard. He knocked on the door and pushed it further open.

103

'Excuse me, but do you know if Miss Epton will be free soon?'

Stephanie gave him a chilly look. 'Is your friend getting impatient?'

'He's a bit pushed for time,' Fox said with a placatory smile.

'So are Mr Snaith and Miss Epton.'

'It's only Miss Epton we've come to see.'

'Who you've come to see and who you actually see can be two different things,' Stephanie retorted. A light blinked on the switchboard and she inserted a plug. A moment later, she turned to Fox and said, 'They're ready to see you now. Better fetch your friend from the waiting-room.'

Fox felt put out by her whole tone and demeanour. Guilt by association, that's what it was working with D.I. Dormer.

On entering Rosa's office, Dormer gave her a curt nod and then stared in hostile fashion at Robin.

'This is my partner, Mr Snaith,' Rosa said. 'He's going to sit in on the interview.'

Dormer seemed about to protest, but ended up saying nothing. Meanwhile, Rosa cast a small smile in the direction of D.C. Fox who was hovering behind his detective inspector. She motioned them to chairs and sat down behind her desk with Robin beside her.

It struck her again, as she studied Dormer's face, that his eyes gave him one of the most unfriendly expressions she had ever seen. His mouth might sometimes be contorted into a smile, but there would be no co-operation from his eyes.

He was dressed in a suit of clerical grey which had seen better days and had a grey striped shirt and a red tie with an indecipherable emblem on it. She reflected that the Metropolitan Police tended to strike new ties like commemorative coins.

D.C. Fox sat on a hard upright chair with pen poised over his pocket-book which lay smoothed open on his knee.

'I'm investigating a very serious matter,' Dormer said in a rasping voice. 'Namely that you and Nash conspired together

104

to pervert the course of justice by interfering with a prosecution witness in the rape case brought against Nash.'

He paused and looked at Rosa.

'If that's a question,' she said, 'the answer is rubbish.'

'Do you admit that you and Miss Langley spoke together on the phone after the case had started?'

'She telephoned me to my considerable embarrassment.'

'Was that when you first advised her against giving evidence?'

'On the contrary, I told her I couldn't discuss the case with her as we were in opposite camps.'

'But, nevertheless, you did discuss it?'

'We did not. I told her she should refer her doubts to you.'

'Doubts? What doubts?'

'Her doubts about pursuing the case against Nash, of course. That was why she phoned me in the first place. She was very upset that he'd been remanded in custody. She said she'd never intended the matter to get that far and that she'd merely wanted to teach him a lesson.'

'A lesson for what?' Dormer barked.

'Not for raping her, if that's what you're thinking.'

'For what, then?'

'He'd upset her.'

'Of course he'd upset her, he'd raped her.'

Rosa shook her head wearily as though trying to reason with a particularly obtuse child.

'As you very well know, Inspector, this case was going to be fought all the way. I'm confident that my client would have been honourably discharged in the magistrates' court. I regret that Miss Langley's death has reduced that to a mere formality.'

'In my view, your client had an excellent motive for murdering Miss Langley.'

'That's a perversion of the truth. You know as well as I do that Miss Langley had been back-tracking almost from the first moment. Any other police officer would have recognised it and accepted the inevitable. I assume it was your personal vanity that prevented you from doing so.'

105

'Are you suggesting I had personal motives for keeping the case alive?' he asked furiously.

'Miss Epton's not suggesting any such thing,' Robin broke in quickly. 'Why don't you confine your questions to what's strictly relevant to your investigation?'

'I don't need a lecture from you on how to perform my duty. Your partner is in a very vulnerable position and knows it.' He turned his attention back to Rosa. 'Is it not a fact that you had dinner with Nash last Friday?'

'Yes, I did,' Rosa replied with a note of challenge.

'Do you often dine out with your clients? Particularly those charged with rape?' he asked with a sneer.

'You're overlooking the fact that I first met Toby Nash on a social occasion. That was how we came to know each other.'

Dormer's expression was scornful and Rosa sat tensely wondering whether he was going to probe further the evening she and Toby spent together. When he glanced up from the sheet of paper he held in his hand, it was to set off on a fresh tack.

'Are you aware that Nash phoned Miss Langley after the last court hearing?'

'Yes.'

'Was that at your instigation?'

'Certainly not. You will recall that I gave an undertaking in court and I also warned my client afterwards not to get in touch with her.'

'So he went against your advice?'

'Yes.'

'It could be, of course, that you aided and abetted him; that it was a further part of your conspiracy to interfere with the course of justice.'

'I've already told you there was no conspiracy and no attempt to interfere with your witness.'

He reminded her of a heavy locomotive that could only move forward and only on its predestined course. The sheet of paper in his hand was obviously some form of *aide-mémoire*. Rosa thought he had probably written out the questions in advance and was methodically working his way down the list.

106

The hapless D.C. Fox was, meanwhile scrawling away furiously in his notebook as he sought futilely to keep up.

Without underestimating Dormer, Rosa was feeling more confident than she had been at the outset of the interview. Surely it must be clear to everyone in the room that he had got nowhere with his questions. Indeed, on reflection, she couldn't think how he'd ever expected to. He had been all bark and no bite.

'You understand that I shall want to see you again,' he now said abruptly. 'The matter is by no means closed.'

'Are you part of the team investigating the murder?' Robin asked, curiously.

'Detective Superintendent Savill has borrowed my services in view of the close connection between my rape case and the murder.'

'There may turn out to be no connection at all,' Robin said.

Dormer, who was by the door, turned and gave him a hard stare. A couple of seconds later his footsteps echoed heavily along the corridor.

In a slightly puzzled tone, Robin said, 'He's obviously not stupid and yet there were times when he gave that impression.'

'He's never struck me as having an exactly quicksilver mind,' Rosa said disdainfully.

'I agree. I'd say animal cunning was more his strong suit.'

'I still find him an utterly objectionable man.'

Robin nodded. 'Not likeable at all. And dangerous, too.'

Rosa was thoughtful for a moment. 'I'm not sure I shan't start mounting a counter-attack,' she said, giving her partner a challenging look. 'It's always been the best form of defence.'

'Be careful, Rosa, that's all! Don't lose your cool and stir up a hornets nest!'

Her smile turned into a sly grin. 'Don't worry, Robin, my counter-attack won't be heralded by trumpets and a cavalry charge. It'll be conducted with stealth.'

CHAPTER 14

Detective Superintendent Savill was used to getting very little sleep during the early stages of a murder enquiry and often going without any on the first night. On this occasion, he did, however, get to bed around three o'clock, if only to get up again at seven.

There was rarely much to show for all the early toil, but it was, nevertheless, a vital period in any investigation and one during which the ground was, so to speak, staked out.

Before he did get to bed that Sunday night, he met Tricia's father who had driven up to London immediately on hearing the news. Although he arrived only shortly before midnight, he said he had no desire to hang around London and proposed driving back home as soon as the purpose of his visit had been accomplished.

He was a tall, thin man with an austere face, who was also sparing of words.

He accompanied Savill to the mortuary for which the superintendent had had to borrow the key to gain admittance.

'Yes, that's Tricia,' he said unemotionally when Savill showed him the body.

Afterwards, despite his impatience to get away, he did accept the offer of a cup of coffee and a sandwich before starting on his journey home.

'When did you last see your daughter, Mr Langley?' Savill asked as they sat in his office which looked at its drabbest at one o'clock in the morning.

'She was home for a few days over Christmas.'

'Would you have any idea who might have killed her?'

'None.' In a severe tone, he added, 'We didn't know any of her London friends.'

'I gather she was once engaged to a young man named Peter Rossington. Did you ever meet him?'

'No.'

'But you did know she was engaged?'

'What does the word mean these days? There was certainly never any formal engagement as there used to be in my young days.'

'Did you know much about the sort of life she lived in London?'

'Precious little. She knew where her home was and that she could always turn to us in time of trouble. But she was a self-possessed girl and at twenty-six her life was hers to make the best of.'

'What it comes to, Mr Langley, is that you left her to live her life without parental interference.'

'Exactly.'

'Forgive my asking you this, but do you have any knowledge of her sex life?'

'None at all.'

'The post mortem examination has revealed that she wasn't a virgin.'

'I imagine very few girls of her age are these days,' he said with a dismissive sniff.

Savill decided not to tell him that, in the view of the pathologist, she was someone to whom sexual intercourse was likely to have been physically painful. Further tests were still required to ascertain whether such had taken place shortly before her death.

With Mr Langley showing increasing signs of impatience to be on his way, Savill thanked him for coming and accompanied him out to his car.

'At least, it's a nice dry night,' he remarked.

'I enjoy night driving,' Mr Langley said. 'I'll be home around dawn.'

Savill's final act before taking himself off to bed was to arrange for Detective Sergeant Speed to call at Tricia's place of employment as soon as the office opened on Monday morning.

109

M.E. (Consultants) Ltd was located on the first floor of a modern building five minutes walk from Victoria Station.

It had a small entrance lobby carpeted in Burgundy red, where a reception desk stood guard over the passage leading to the various offices.

It was all flimsy partitioning and bright colours and artfully concealed lighting.

The reception desk was unattended when Sergeant Speed walked through the entrance door, but he could hear voices coming from one of the rooms along the passage.

He was looking round for a bell (scuffing his shoes on the floor, his usual way of attracting attention, would have been a waste of time) when a girl popped out of one of the rooms and came hurrying toward him.

'I'm terribly sorry,' she said. 'I hope you haven't been waiting long. We're all in a state this morning. Mr Harris' secretary was found murdered over the weekend.'

'I know. That's why I'm here. I'm Detective Sergeant Speed. I'd like to speak to Mr Harris.'

The girl gave him a startled look and then darted off along the passage, disappearing through the end door on the left.

While waiting for her to reappear, he became aware of another door opening and an older woman taking a furtive look at him.

After about three minutes, the door through which the receptionist had gone opened and she was preceded out by a worried looking man in his late thirties. He wasn't wearing a jacket, but his wide striped blue shirt indicated sartorial chic.

'I'm Giles Harris,' he said, holding out his hand. 'Let me take you along to my office. I only heard the news about Tricia when I arrived this morning. One of the clerks had read it in the paper. I still can't take it in.' He closed the door behind Speed and motioned him to a low swivel chair upholstered in a ginger-coloured material. Its angle gave it an abandoned appearance. Speed lowered himself into it carefully, while Giles Harris went round to the other side of his glass-topped desk.

'When did it happen?' he asked, offering Speed a cigarette.

110

'We think she was probably killed on Friday evening, but her body wasn't discovered until yesterday.'

'Poor girl! Have you made an arrest yet?'

'No.'

'What was it, a sex crime?'

'Why do you ask that?' Speed said suspiciously.

Giles Harris removed his heavy horn-rimmed spectacles and massaged the bridge of his nose.

'She was a very attractive girl and I always felt she had a bit of the femme fatale about her.' Quickly he added, 'Not that she was my type. Indeed, her private life was a closed book as far as I was concerned.'

'How long had she been your secretary?'

'Almost a year.'

'Good at her job?'

'Very, when she wanted to be. But she was apt to take liberties with office time. She definitely put her own interests before those of her employer.'

'I'm surprised you kept her in the circumstances.'

Harris gave a helpless shrug. 'As I've said, she was excellent on her day and, anyway, efficient secretaries don't come with the groceries. Though recently I had been wondering whether to make a change. She'd been taking days off at most inconvenient times for various undisclosed reasons.'

'Any idea who might have killed her?'

'None.'

'Nobody here?'

'Good gracious, no!'

'How many people do you employ?'

'There's me and my partner for a start, our two secretaries –well, one secretary now– Annabel, the receptionist, two young clerks, both male, and Miss Wyngard, who's the cashier cum book-keeper cum accountant. She's been here for years. Indeed, we took her over when we bought what was then a moribund business fifteen years ago. I'm happy to say it's now a flourishing one with a very creditable turnover for its size.'

A few minutes later, Speed got up to leave.

111

'If anything occurs to you which might assist our enquiries, will you give me a call, Mr Harris?'

'Certainly I will.' He shook his head unhappily. 'I suppose I shall have to write a letter of condolence to her parents, not that I've ever met them. And, of course, a wreath will be sent on behalf of the staff. Do you have any idea when and where the funeral will be held?'

'Afraid not. Depends on how soon the coroner releases the body.'

As he opened the door of Giles Harris' office, he was sure that one further down on the other side of the passage was softly closed. It was the door round which a woman had earlier peered at him. It had to be Miss Wyngard.

It was not until Monday evening that Superintendent Savill next saw Inspector Dormer. He had been waiting to hear from him all day and had begun to be exasperated by his elusiveness.

'Well,' he said in a distinctly cool tone, 'what happened when you went to see Nash last night?'

'He'll crack in due course,' Dormer remarked, unabashed by the other's tone. 'All I need is a bit of leverage.'

'You're still certain he's the man?'

'He sticks out like a lighthouse. Who had a better motive to murder her than Nash?'

'I don't see that,' Savill said. 'From all I hear, she was about to fold as a witness anyway, so why did he have to kill her?'

Dormer frowned. 'I don't know where you got that from, sir. I'm confident I could still have got her to give evidence. That's what Nash was afraid of and that's why he killed her.'

'That's not Mr Gilman's view.'

'Oh! So that's who you've been talking to! He only saw her in court that once. The trouble with Miss Langley was that she could be too easily swayed. I ought to have got her away from that flat and put her somewhere out of reach until she'd given her evidence. Then there wouldn't have been all this trouble and she'd still be alive.'

'I obviously ought to see Nash myself,' Savill said, thoughtfully. 'Meanwhile, I shall keep an open mind. I agree Nash must be seen as a suspect, but so, in my view, must that landlord and Rossington whom we're still trying to trace.'

'What did the p.m. reveal?' Dormer enquired.

'That somebody may have tried to have intercourse with her, but was unsuccessful in the sense that no semen was found in her.'

'That shows it wasn't a sex murder at all. The murderer just made it look that way to mislead us. The motive was quite different.' He threw Savill a challenging look.

'Bringing us back to Nash, you mean?'

'Precisely.'

'I'm not saying you mayn't be right, but I'm still keeping other possibilities in mind.' After a pause, he asked, 'What about Nash's solicitor? Do you really believe she had a hand in trying to persuade Tricia Langley not to give evidence?'

'I'm sure of it. Her relations with Nash go far beyond those of solicitor and client. I've now found out they've been socialising together since the case began, which strikes me as a scandalous state of affairs. I interviewed her at her office this afternoon. She denied everything I put to her, but that was to be expected. Once I crack Nash, however, I'll be well on the way to getting her. When are you proposing to see Nash, sir?'

'As soon as possible.'

'If you take my advice, you'll have him along to the station.'

'I'll think about it.'

'I take it you'll want me to be present?'

'I'll let you know later.'

Dormer scowled. 'When are you expecting to hear something from forensic?'

'They've promised to let me have a preliminary report on the phone tomorrow. I had to pull a few strings to get some priority.'

'Let's hope they provide the leverage we need to crack the case.'

'Yes, let's hope!' Savill said abstractedly.

He actually brought himself to address me as 'sir' a couple of times, he reflected wryly after D.I. Dormer had departed.

'Oh, you answer it,' Sara said with a touch of asperity when the phone rang for the umpteenth time on Monday evening. 'It's sure to be the press again.'

'I thought you didn't like me talking to the press,' Janice said. 'That's what you told me a short while ago.'

The truth was that both of them had begun to react against the events of the past twenty-four hours and were on edge. It was in this mood that Sara had reproached Janice for talking too freely to the press, saying that she didn't think it seemly to regale them with so many personal details of their lives. Janice, stung by this observation, had retorted that it was better than having them invent a whole lot of lurid details.

'You can answer it without pouring out your soul,' Sara replied tetchily.

'If I answer it, I do it in my own way,' Janice said in a stubborn tone. Then looking at her friend, she exclaimed, 'If we go on like this, we'll soon be throwing the furniture at each other.'

Sara nodded ruefully. 'Yes, I'm sorry,' she said to Janice's retreating back.

From what she heard of the ensuing conversation, Janice was agreeing to somebody coming round to see them. She assumed it was one of the police officers coming back to clear up some point or other.

'Who was it?' she asked when Janice returned to the room.

'Rosa Epton.'

'Not a reporter?' Sara cried in a tone of alarm.

'No, a solicitor. Toby Nash's solicitor to be precise.'

'What on earth does she want?'

'She merely said she'd be grateful if she could come round for a chat. She sounded rather nice. I've asked her for coffee. She'll be here in about half an hour.'

Sara let out a sigh. 'I suppose we'd better clear away the supper things. I used to think all female solicitors resembled middle-aged school marms until I met the sister of one of my brother's friends. She was terribly pretty. Did this Epton woman sound old?'

Janice nodded. 'All of our age, I'd say!'

When she arrived, Rosa was wearing a pair of jeans and an enveloping blue sweater.

'I came as I was,' she said with a smile. 'Quite frankly, I rang you on the spur of the moment and was most grateful when you said I could come round at once.'

'What do you wear in court?' Sara asked with interest while Janice went to fetch the coffee.

'I have an assortment of basically black outfits, not because they look legal, though I suppose they do, but because they don't show the dirt. Some courts are dirtier than going down a mine.'

Janice returned bearing a tray of coffee mugs which she set down on the table.

'Help yourself to milk or sugar,' she said.

Rosa took a mug and glanced round the room. 'It reminds me of the days when I used to share,' she said. 'Except there were five of us. Four girls and a boy. He was gay and quite the least trouble of anyone. But it was just like living in a transit camp. I couldn't wait to get a place of my own.'

'I know how you must have felt,' Janice remarked. 'I think there's a time limit to this sort of life. I'm not sure I haven't reached it.'

'We're going to have difficulty filling Tricia's room,' Sara said, after a pause.

'I don't think there'll be any problem at all,' Janice remarked. 'Its curiosity value may even enable us to get a larger contribution toward the rent.'

'What a ghoulish thought!' Sara said.

The two girls now turned and looked at Rosa as if signalling her to state her business.

Pushing back her hair which had fallen forward on either side of her face, Rosa began.

'I was Toby Nash's solicitor in the rape case which involved Tricia. With her death, that's come to an end, but the police officer concerned seems intent on proving that Toby killed her

115

after he and I had tried to persuade her not to give evidence against him.'

'Is that the sour-faced officer who was here when we arrived back yesterday evening?' Janice asked. 'Was it really only yesterday evening?' she went on, shaking her head disbelievingly.

'His name's Detective Inspector Dormer,' Rosa said.

'The other one's much nicer. The rather dishy superintendent.'

'There's nothing nice about Detective Inspector Dormer,' Rosa observed. Looking at the two girls, she went on, 'I gather Tricia never mentioned what happened on New Year's Eve?'

'Not a word,' Janice said. 'We didn't know a thing until the police told us.'

'When you went off this last weekend leaving her on her own here, did she say what her plans were?'

This time it was Sara who answered. 'No. We asked her to visit Miss Greenwood who's blind and lives in the flat below, but she didn't seem too keen on the idea. But whether that was because she had other plans or couldn't be bothered, I don't know.'

'As far as you're aware she wasn't expecting any visitors on Friday evening?'

'That's what the police wanted to know. She never mentioned any.'

'Had she mentioned Toby recently?'

'Only the other evening when he phoned and I picked up the receiver and thought I recognised his voice and asked her afterwards if it was him. I must say she gave him a bit of a brush off that evening. They weren't talking for more than a minute.'

'It was naughty of him to have called her,' Rosa said. 'However, she didn't give any indication of being frightened of him?'

'Of Toby?' Janice asked in a tone of surprise. 'Nobody could be afraid of Toby.'

'From which I gather you don't regard him as a suspect?'

'Good gracious, no!'

116

'But somebody murdered Tricia.'

'Janice and I think it might have been nosy Norm. He's our landlord and lives in the basement flat.'

'What about Peter Rossington?'

'I hope it wasn't him,' Janice said. 'I've always liked Peter, even if he can behave a bit oddly at times. I wonder if the police have found him yet ... '

It was about fifteen minutes later after they had exchanged further views that Rosa said with a sigh, 'Tricia seems to have been something of an enigma.'

'That's one word for her,' Janice remarked acidly. 'I know one doesn't speak ill of the dead, and at least this is not maliciously said, but she was basically a selfish person. She treated people rather as a cat does. As conveniences of the moment.'

Suddenly the telephone rang and Janice went off to answer it. She closed the door behind her and it was several minutes before she returned. When she did so, she was wearing a puzzled frown.

'That was a very odd conversation,' she observed.

'Who was it?'

'That woman where Tricia worked. Joyce Wyngard.'

'What did she want?'

'That's what was so odd. I've no idea and she didn't seem to know either. She kept on saying how shocked she'd been by the news and whom did we suspect? At least, that's what it seemed to come to in the end.'

'What did you tell her?'

'I told her we were also shocked and that we were completely in the dark as to who had done it.'

'What did she sound like?'

'Like someone who's mislaid their head.'

'Tricia couldn't stand her,' Sara explained to Rosa. 'She's one of these keep-fit fanatics.'

Not long after this, Rosa took her leave. Though she had learnt little that was new, she was well satisfied with her visit. She felt she had forged a friendly link with Janice and Sara and could regard them as allies.

117

Rosa could hear her telephone ringing before she opened the front-door. She hoped it would cease before she reached it, but it didn't. Instinct gave her a shrewd idea as to who her caller was. Reluctantly she lifted the receiver.

'Rosa, darling, I've been trying to get you all evening,' Philippa said in a gush. 'Where've you been?'

'I've only just this minute walked in.'

'I didn't ring you at your office because Adrian told me not to, so I waited until I thought you'd be home.'

'What can I do for you?' Rosa asked crisply.

'Do for me! You sound like the complaints department at Harrods, except you didn't say madam. What you can do for me, darling, is tell me who's suspected of murdering Tricia? I gather the police haven't yet arrested anybody.'

'Not as far as I know.'

'So who's under suspicion?'

'I can't say.'

'Oh, Rosa darling, don't be so uptight. I'm a friend.'

'Even so, you must realise I can't discuss something like this over the telephone.'

'Then we must meet,' Philippa said promptly. 'Come to dinner tomorrow evening and tell all. I promise not to ask anybody else. It'll just be you and me and Adrian.'

Plus half a dozen of your closest friends, Rosa thought, and then immediately felt ashamed.

'Everything's in such a state of flux at the moment, it's better if I don't make any firm dates. But I'll hope to see you before long, Philippa.'

'Well, darling, if you won't, you won't and I can hear Adrian muttering in the background that I mustn't twist your arm. But promise you'll get in touch with me soon.'

Rosa promised and gratefully rang off. She could almost hear Philippa saying to her friends, 'We've had a murder in the family. Our first!'

Detective Superintendent Savill decided that he wanted to

make his own assessment of Toby and that he wanted to do so without the inhibiting presence of D.I. Dormer.

He agreed with Dormer on one point, namely that the best venue for such interviews was a police station. He was aware, however, that Toby was likely to demur strongly at this suggestion and would probably start shouting for his solicitor. And Savill no more wanted Rosa to be present than he did Dormer.

He had come across her on a few occasions and respected her professional ability. He had never regarded her as coming within the category of crooked lawyer and this made him question Dormer's judgment of her. If, of course, she was having an affair with Nash, as Dormer had hinted, then he supposed that she might have behaved with impulsive stupidity in an effort to save him from the consequences of his own conduct.

In any event, there was only one way to resolve such speculative issues and that was by seeing Nash and making up his own mind about him. He hoped he would then know where to place him on his short-list of suspects.

Toby was taking a shower when the phone rang. He hadn't got back from work until just before eight o'clock – well, from the pub where he had been drinking with friends for a couple of hours after leaving the bank.

Sam was out to dinner and he was proposing to grill bacon and sausages for his supper and settle down in front of the telly for the remainder of the evening. Drink had made him feel temporarily carefree. Indeed, D.I. Dormer's ogrelike shape had dissolved with every pint he'd put away.

'Toby Nash here,' he said cheerfully as he lifted the receiver with his free hand, the other clutching a towel to himself.

'If it's not too inconvenient, I'd like to come and see you, Mr Nash. My name's Savill and I'm the officer in charge of enquiries into Miss Langley's death.'

Toby let go of the towel as if it had caught fire. In an agitated voice, he said, 'I'm afraid it's not convenient and, anyway, my solicitor has told me not to talk to the police without her being present.'

'I have to see you sometime in the very near future, Mr Nash, and it occurred to me that you might prefer it if I came to you rather than had you along to the station.'

The man's voice was pleasant and his tone persuasive. And there was certainly no jangle of handcuffs to be heard in the background.

'I was interviewed yesterday evening, why's it necessary to see me again?' Toby asked cautiously.

'That was Inspector Dormer. He and I are tackling different angles and I need to see you myself.'

'Are you an inspector too?'

'No, I'm a superintendent. Now if it's convenient I can be with you within half an hour. I have your address and I know the road quite well as I had an aunt who used to live there.'

In Savill's experience there was nothing like a homely touch for gaining someone's confidence. It was a lesson Dormer would never learn.

A policeman with an aunt who used to live in this road, Toby thought. He must be all right.

As soon as Savill had rung off, Toby tried to call Rosa. But her number rang and rang without answer. He was to go on calling her without success until the moment of Savill's arrival. He had no way of knowing she had gone round to Tricia's flat.

His first impression of Savill was that he looked as agreeable as he had sounded.

'Like a beer?' Toby asked a trifle diffidently as he led the way into the ever untidy living-room.

'No thank you, Mr Nash.'

'A coffee, then?

'Not even coffee.' It was premature to accept even minor hospitality from somebody who might turn out to be Tricia Langley's murderer.

He watched Toby covertly while he opened a can of beer for himself and poured it out. He looked an amiable young man, but Savill had been a policeman for too long to be taken in by looks.

'Let me come to the point straight away, Mr Nash. Would you mind telling me your movements last Friday evening?'
'I had dinner with a friend.'
'Was that Miss Epton?'
Toby nodded. 'Yes, we went to a little Italian restaurant called *Il Trovatore* near South Ken station.'
'What time were you there?'
'I called for Rosa – that's Miss Epton – soon after half past seven. I'd booked a table for eight.'
'And what time did you leave the restaurant?'
'Around half past ten. I drove Rosa home and went up to her flat for a nightcap.'
'How long did you stay there?'
Toby shifted uncomfortably. 'It was quite a while. We sat talking and the time just went.'
Savill seemed satisfied with the answer and, to Toby's relief, didn't probe it.
'What were you doing between six o'clock and just after half past seven when you picked up Miss Epton?'
Toby blinked at him in surprise. 'I wasn't doing anything in particular. I was at home until I left about seven fifteen.'
'Alone?'
'Yes.'
'You didn't go and visit any friends?'
'No,' Toby said in a puzzled voice.
'I believe you phoned Miss Langley an evening or two before her death?'
'Yes. It was bloody silly of me. It was the same day as the last court hearing. I wanted to try and make things up with her.'
Savill frowned. 'But she was giving evidence against you on a rape charge and you'd undertaken not to get in touch with her.'
'I know, but it was so obvious she didn't want to go on with the case and she'd hated every second she'd been in the witness box that morning. I just ... well, I felt sorry for her.'
'And that's why you breached a solemn undertaking and called her?'

121

'I assure you it was the only reason,' Toby said in a pleading tone, at the same time reflecting that Superintendent Savill wasn't entirely sugar and spice and all things nice.

'You didn't have a very long conversation, I gather?'

'No. She sounded somewhat hostile and I decided to ring off.'

'Hostile, was she? You mean she was in no mood to accept the olive branch you were tendering?'

'All I mean is that she seemed embarrassed and didn't want to talk,' Toby said in a slightly flustered tone.

'You said hostile, which isn't the same thing.'

'I just don't want to give a wrong impression.'

'What impression do you want to give?' Savill asked, fixing Toby with a steady look.

'Merely that she didn't want to talk.'

'Not that she sounded hostile?'

'No.'

'I wonder then why you chose that word in the first instance.'

'I quite often pick the wrong word.'

Savill raised one eyebrow in an expression of polite doubt.

'Of course, if she *had* sounded hostile, you'd have felt rather worried.'

'I don't think so. Why?'

'Because it might have indicated she was still intent on giving evidence against you.'

'Definitely not. You only had to see her in court.'

'But she could have changed her mind by evening. I gather she was easily swayed. I can't think why else she should have sounded hostile when you called her.'

'She wasn't hostile.'

'It was your word, Mr Nash.'

'But I've explained,' Toby said in an agitated tone while Saville observed him with a dispassionate air.

'Of course, if you were sufficiently worried by her attitude, you'd have wanted to try and swing her back your way again, wouldn't you?' Toby appeared mesmerised by the quiet flow of words. 'A visit, perhaps, where a phone call had failed. A visit on Friday evening when she'd be alone at the flat.'

Jerked into life again, Toby said defiantly, 'If you're so clever, tell me how I'd have known she would be alone?'

'But you knew the other two girls always went away at weekends and that Miss Langley usually remained at the flat.' He gave Toby a smile. 'I hope I can be cleverer than that, Mr Nash.'

'Are you seriously suggesting that I went to her flat on Friday evening and murdered her?'

'All I'm saying is that you could have done so and that a motive has come from your own lips.'

'But I was having dinner with Rosa that evening.'

'You've told me you didn't pick her up until after half past seven.'

'What time was Tricia murdered?' Toby asked in a frantic voice.

'The pathologist finds it difficult to pinpoint a time, but the lady in the flat beneath heard two sets of footsteps overhead between seven and seven thirty and my guess is that one of them belonged to the murderer.'

Toby looked stunned. 'I didn't kill her. I swear I didn't kill her,' he said hoarsely.

'I believe Peter Rossington is a cousin of yours?' Savill said, as if they were enjoying an exchange of social gossip. Toby nodded dully. 'Have you any idea where I can find him?'

'He's always moving around.'

'He's not been in touch with you since Miss Langley's death?'

'No.'

'Where's his home?'

'His father's dead. His mother's remarried and lives in Spain.'

'Has he any brothers or sisters?'

'No.'

'Who are his friends? He has to be somewhere. Somebody must be giving him shelter.'

'He's probably taken a room in bedsitter land.'

'If he does get in touch with you, will you let me know? You see, at this stage of an enquiry, it's a question of trying to eliminate all the possible suspects.'

Or nail them to the floor, Toby thought bitterly. He watched Superintendent Savill get up and brush down the front of his jacket with his hands.

'I'm afraid I shall almost certainly need to see you again, Mr Nash.'

'Next time I shall insist on having my solicitor present,' Toby said aggressively.

Savill appeared to give this judicial consideration before replying.

'Us poor old bobbies, we can hardly talk to anyone these days without a solicitor being present. Hampered the way we are at every turn of an investigation, it's a marvel we ever bring anyone to court.' He gave Toby a rueful grin. 'Anyway, Mr Nash, thank you for a helpful chat this evening. I personally hope you won't remain on my list of suspects for long, but that depends on matters beyond my control.'

CHAPTER 15

Janice and Sara felt that they ran the gauntlet each time they left or entered the house. Nosy Norm was always ready to pounce on them and appeared to track their arrivals and departures with the efficiency of advanced radar.

On Wednesday morning he suddenly popped out of the shadows and confronted them at the bottom of the stairs which they were descending on tiptoe.

'I've just been checking that everything's all right in the Guptas' flat,' he said without a blush. He quickly went on, 'Have you heard anything further from the police?'

'Nope,' Janice said. 'And I can't stop now or I'll be late for work. Come on Sara!'

Sara, however, had been taken by surprise and was embarrassed at being caught tiptoeing down the stairs like a truant. In the second that she paused in hesitation, the landlord had moved to cut off her advance to the front-door.

'What do you think, Miss Fitch? Do you think there'll be an arrest quite soon?'

Sara gave a nervous laugh. 'It's no good asking me. I've no idea.'

'I thought the police might have told you whom they suspect.'

Sara shook her head in a further onrush of embarrassment. 'They've told us nothing,' she stammered.

Janice, who had reached the pavement, now returned up the front steps to the door.

'Are you coming or not, Sara?' she called out.

'Yes, coming,' Sara called back, giving Norman a small helpless smile as she fled past him.

'Once 'you paused, you were sunk,' Janice said in an

125

admonishing tone as they half-walked, half-ran toward the bus stop.

'I felt embarrassed that he caught us tiptoeing down the stairs.'

'He was the one who should have felt embarrassed, lying in wait for us like that.'

'We shall have to leave earlier to avoid him and vary our times.'

'I don't propose to do anything of the sort,' Janice remarked. 'In future I shall completely ignore him. I won't even mumble good morning.' She paused. 'With luck, the police will find that he did it and then he'll be arrested.'

Sara said nothing, but couldn't help feeling this was a rather simplistic solution to the problem.

After their departure, Norman returned to his own flat, rather like a spider retreating to its command post on the perimeter of its web. He knew that the police regarded him as a suspect and it was knowledge that made him extremely uneasy. He longed to be assured that he had been cleared of all suspicion, but, until then, anxiety would continue to gnaw at his vitals.

Like many in the same situation, he was ready to clutch at any straw, however insubstantial. He was certain that whereas he was excluded from the confidence of the police, it was something enjoyed by Sara and Janice. Hence his endeavour to wheedle information from them.

When he had finished washing up his breakfast things (one plate, one knife and one mug), he decided he would go and see Miss Greenwood in flat 3. He had always stood in slight awe of her and normally confined his visits to rent-collecting and the occasions when she would summon him on the phone to attend to something for which he was responsible as landlord.

However, he had not been in touch with her since Tricia's death and that gave him the excuse for a visit now.

He knocked on her front-door and then called out as he always did, 'It's Mr Oliver, Miss Greenwood.'

A couple of minutes later, the door opened and she stood there facing him. She was a short, delicate-boned woman with

126

snow-white hair and pink cheeks, who looked a picture of health. She always wore a pair of dark glasses that shut out all light from her sightless eyes.

'May I come in for a few minutes, Miss Greenwood?' he asked with an ingratiating smile that she was spared seeing. 'I've not talked to you since the tragedy upstairs and I thought I'd come up and make sure you're all right.'

'Yes, come in,' she said, conscious of the fact that it had taken three days for him to show his solicitude. She didn't mind this, but she had always despised cant.

'I hope you haven't been too upset by all the happenings,' he went on, reciprocating the distasteful stare bestowed on him by her cat, Jasper.

'Have the police yet caught the man?' Miss Greenwood asked, ignoring his remark.

'Not that I've heard. I was wondering if they might have told you something.'

'Why on earth should they?' she asked sharply.

'They might have hinted to you whom they were looking for.'

Miss Greenwood frowned. Her ears told her that her landlord was a worried man and she wondered why.

'I'm sure the police wouldn't be so foolish,' she said in a dismissive tone. 'I like to believe that they keep their suspicions to themselves. In any event, the only police officer who's visited me was Detective Sergeant Speed on Sunday evening.'

'I don't suppose you were able to tell him very much, were you?'

'I told him what I could,' she replied.

If Norman was hoping to learn what she had said, he was to be disappointed.

'Have Miss Turnbull or Miss Fitch been to visit you since it all happened?'

'Of course they have. They're two very kind and considerate girls,' she said pointedly.

'Well, I'm glad that events haven't got you down,' the landlord said, casting Jasper another look of disfavour. But this time the cat was asleep and didn't return it. 'If there's nothing I can do, I'll leave you in peace.'

Miss Greenwood made no effort to detain him and a few minutes later he was back in his own flat with his sense of uneasiness increased rather than assuaged.

It was about half an hour after his return downstairs that a car pulled up outside and he saw Detective Superintendent Savill and Detective Sergeant Holthouse get out. He quickly stepped back from the window as they came down the basement steps.

'Good morning, Mr Oliver. May we come in?' Savill said when the door opened. For a few seconds, however, Norman stood staring at his visitors without moving. 'You seem surprised to see us.'

Norman let out a not very convincing laugh. 'I was expecting to find the milkman when I opened the door.'

Savill and Sergeant Holthouse, who had spotted Norman before he ducked away from the window, exchanged sardonic glances.

'How's your investigation going?' Norman went on as he closed the front door behind them.

'It's going,' Savill said laconically.

'Are you confident of making an arrest?' Norman asked in a nervously eager tone.

'Oh, I shall make an arrest all right.'

'Does that mean you know who you're looking for?'

'I hope to very soon. Which brings me to the reason for this visit. I'd like to have a sample of your hair. Your head hair.'

If he had stuck a darning needle into Norman's ample behind, he couldn't have achieved greater shock. The landlord gave a startled yelp and a hand flew up to his head as if to make sure it was still there.

'What do you want my hair for?' he asked in alarm.

'Don't look so worried, Mr Oliver,' Savill said with a laugh. 'I'm not after all of it. Just two or three hairs as a sample.'

'But what for?'

'To compare with a hair found on Miss Langley's pillow. A hair which is not one of hers.'

128

Norman stared at his visitors with a trapped expression.

'You think I murdered her,' he shouted. 'I know you do. But I didn't.'

'Just calm down,' Savill said peaceably. 'Yours is not the only sample we're seeking.' He gazed at Norman's rather greasy, indeterminate-coloured hair. 'Now if you're agreeable, Sergeant Holthouse will pluck two or three hairs from different parts of your head and we'll send them to the laboratory in a sealed bag. It'll be quite painless. Nothing like as nasty as going to the dentist.'

'And if I don't agree?' Norman said in a tense voice.

'We'll note your refusal to co-operate and get hold of them some other way. But I'm sure you're not going to refuse, are you?'

Sergeant Holthouse, who had taken a pair of tweezers and a plastic envelope from his pocket, moved across to where Norman was sitting. Norman, meanwhile, had tightly closed his eyes and assumed an expression of martyrdom.

When the operation was over, he said in an anxious voice, 'My hair's always falling out. Every time I comb it, some comes out. In fact, you'll find my hairs all over the place.'

'What you're trying to tell me, Mr Oliver, is that, if your hair happens to match the one found on Miss Langley's pillow, I oughtn't to place too much significance on the fact. Am I right?'

Norman gave a nod of obvious relief. 'Yes. For example, I'm constantly brushing hairs off my shoulders. You see, I've suffered from dandruff all my life. I can't tell you how many remedies I've tried, but none of them seem to work.'

'Too bad,' Savill observed. 'But in view of what you say, perhaps you'll tell me when you were last in Miss Langley's bedroom?'

Norman gaped at him. 'Oh ... not for ages. When I go up to their flat, I'm normally only in the hall or the living-room. I have no reason to enter the bedrooms.'

'Isn't there a sashcord in Miss Langley's room that you were anxious to check?'

Norman blinked and turned scarlet.

129

'Yes, now that you remind me, I believe I did mention it to Miss Langley.' He licked his lips which had gone suddenly dry. 'I suppose she must have told the other two?'

'Yes,' Savill said with a nod. 'I'm not an expert, but I've examined the window in question and couldn't find anything wrong with it at all.'

'The sashcord definitely needs renewing,' Norman remarked emphatically.

'Or were you merely seeking an excuse to go into her bedroom?' Savill enquired, fixing him with a hard stare.

'Why should I want to do that?' The question was accompanied by a sickly smile.

Ignoring it, Savill went on, 'I take it you found Miss Langley attractive?'

'As far as I was concerned, she was just one of the girls in the top flat.'

'Now try answering my question!'

'Yes, I suppose she was quite attractive in a way.'

'Don't hedge, Mr Oliver. You were attracted by her, weren't you?'

Norman squirmed. 'All right, she was attractive, if that's what you want me to say.'

'My information is that you were always finding excuses to hang around her.'

'That's a lie,' Norman said excitedly.

'Did you know you had the reputation of being a dirty old man?'

'That's a foul slander ... Just because I've always tried to be a conscientious landlord, vile calumnies are hurled at my head.'

Savill observed him with a thoughtful expression.

'I suppose the two girls have been putting these ideas into your head,' Norman went on in obvious agitation. 'It's a stab in the back after all I've done for them. As far as I'm concerned, the sooner they now leave the better. I never dreamt they'd be capable of such disloyalty.'

'Get down off your high horse,' Savill said amiably. 'It doesn't suit you.' He got up from his chair. 'Once I have the laboratory report on your hair sample, I'll be in touch with you again.'

'I hope you'll remember what I told you about my dropping hairs all over the place,' Norman said in a tone of desperation as he accompanied them to the door.

'Certainly I will, though from what you've said, you couldn't have shed any in Miss Langley's bedroom.'

'No, I couldn't have.'

'And not even you are suggesting that one might have blown in through the window and come to rest on her pillow.'

Norman glared at their backs as they ran up the basement steps and got into their car. He was consumed with a mixture of anger and fear.

'Now to Petersham Magistrates' Court,' Savill said, as Sergeant Holthouse pulled away from the kerb. 'We'll be in time to hear the final chapter of the Nash case – and collect a sample of his hair while we're there.'

CHAPTER 16

Rosa and Toby arrived at court separately. Rosa had deemed this advisable in the circumstances. Even so, she wasn't prepared for the chilliness of her reception.

Gilman, the prosecuting solicitor, gave her a distant nod and the clerk ostentatiously ignored her. It seemed that Inspector Dormer had already injected his poison into them.

Far from feeling abashed, however, Rosa experienced an upsurge of defiance and determination.

Moving along the row toward Gilman, she said, 'May I ask what you're proposing to tell the court about recent events?'

He gave her a tight-lipped look as though he found the question in poor taste.

'I shall merely say that Miss Langley is dead and the subject of a murder investigation and that, as the prosecution is now unable to proceed with the case, I have no alternative but to ask for your client to be discharged.'

Rosa nodded. 'I certainly think it would be undesirable to say more than that.'

Gilman half-turned away to indicate he had no wish to discuss the matter further.

Rosa got up and walked round the end of the row to speak to the clerk, who declined to look up.

Addressing the top of his head, she said, 'I shall be applying for legal aid.'

Slowly he raised his head and stared at her with a portentous frown.

'I can't stop you applying,' he said brusquely.

'I was going to do so on the last occasion, but forgot when the hearing came to its abrupt end.'

'Why do you want to apply now?'

'This is my third appearance in the case and I'm entitled to remuneration.'

'Is your client not able to pay for your services himself?' the clerk asked in an offensive voice.

'I'm not saying that legal aid is automatically granted,' Rosa said stubbornly, 'but I've never known it refused in a rape case.'

The clerk gave a shrug of indifference. 'As I've said, I can't *stop* you applying.'

After Rosa had returned to her seat, she gazed around the court-room. She noticed that the press box was full to overflowing for the first time, Tricia's death having undoubtedly added a new dimension to public interest. She wondered what tendentious titbits Dormer had fed them. Dormer himself was standing beside the witness box with the air of an ill-tempered deity. Sitting nearby was Detective Superintendent Savill, who had obviously just arrived. He put up a hand to smooth down his hair and looked warm as if he'd been running. On the opposite side of the court near to the entrance, she spotted D.C. Fox. She caught his eye and he gave her a fleeting smile. He had better watch out, she thought. Smiling at me is probably a capital offence in Dormer's eyes. Fox generally managed to look uneasy, but today he had a positively hunted appearance.

As she completed her survey of everyone in court, she reflected that the only person she had not seen that morning was her client. But she knew Toby must have arrived and surrendered to his bail or she would have been told. Probably not so much told as accused of having spirited him away.

A few minutes later, however, the magistrates took their seats and Toby was brought into the dock. Rosa turned and gave him a smile of encouragement. She had spoken to him on the phone the previous evening and had told him in general terms what to expect. She had vetoed his suggestion of wearing a black tie, saying that it would strike a false note, which the police would be quick to exploit.

Gilman now rose to his feet and began to address the three magistrates in a sombre voice.

133

'I regret to have to inform the Court that since the last hearing, Miss Patricia Langley has been found dead in her flat. She had been murdered and a full scale investigation is under way, though no arrest has yet been made. In these circumstances, you will understand that I have no option but to ask you to discharge the accused, for without Miss Langley's evidence the charge of rape cannot be sustained. For reasons which you will readily appreciate, it is better that I should say no more than I have.'

As Rosa listened, she couldn't help recalling Robin Snaith's theory that when lawyers said 'for reasons which you will readily appreciate', what they really meant was, either 'my reasons are too dubious to be given' or, 'think of a few reasons for yourself, but don't ask me'.

After Gilman had sat down, the clerk turned and spoke briefly to the chairman of the bench who then addressed Toby.

'The charge against you is dismissed,' he said.

It became suddenly apparent to Rosa that the magistrates were about to leave the bench and she quickly stood up.

'I have an application to make to your worships,' she said in a loud, clear voice. 'I wish to apply for legal aid in respect of the three appearances my client has made in connection with this charge. In my submission, the death of Miss Langley in no way invalidates the application, which is one I should have made today in any event.'

The clerk once more turned and held a whispered colloquy with the bench, though this one lasted considerably longer. When, however, he eventually turned round and faced the court again, Rosa could tell from his displeased expression that her application was going to be granted against his advice.

'We grant your application, Miss Epton,' the chairman said a trifle breathlessly.

As Rosa pushed her way out of court, a number of reporters converged on her.

'Have the police yet interviewed your client about the murder, Miss Epton?' one of them asked.

'All I can tell you is that my client completely denies having had anything to do with Miss Langley's murder.'

'Do the police accept his denial?' another reporter called out as she tried to push past them.

'I have no reason to believe they don't,' she said boldly.

'It has been suggested that somebody tried to persuade Tricia Langley not to give evidence and then killed her when she refused to agree.'

Rosa halted and turned toward the reporter who had spoken.

'I know of no such somebody,' she said in a stinging tone. 'And I'd advise you to be extremely careful what you print to that effect.'

The reporter gave her a knowing wink and went on his way.

As Rosa began looking round the lobby for Toby, D.C. Fox appeared suddenly at her side.

'Can you come across to the station, Miss Epton? Detective Superintendent Savill would like to have a word with you.'

'All right, but do you know where Nash has got to?'

'He's with Mr Savill,' Fox said with a nervous gulp.

Rosa was about to remonstrate, but realised there was no point in attacking the unfortunate D.C. Fox. It would be better to wait and find out what Savill wanted and what Toby was doing at the police station. Of one thing she was sure, he hadn't gone there of his own volition.

'How's life under Inspector Dormer?' she asked, as they stood waiting to cross the road. 'Still as challenging as ever?'

'It's nothing to joke about, Miss Epton,' he said in an almost piteous tone. Then in a conspiratorial whisper, he added, 'He's out to get you and Nash.'

'I'm well aware of it. He's never troubled to hide the fact.'

'Don't underestimate him!'

'Why are you telling me this?' Rosa asked curiously.

'Because I don't believe Nash ever raped Tricia Langley. He may have had an aggressive fumble, but don't tell me he had intercourse with her without her consent, which is what the law says. But the D.I. can never admit he's wrong.'

135

'Do *you* believe that Nash and I tried to dissuade her from giving evidence?'

He threw her a scared look. 'I oughtn't to have said what I did. Promise you won't use it against me?'

'I shan't grass on you. But you didn't answer my question.'

'What I believe is neither here nor there. The D.I. doesn't listen to the likes of me.' In a strangulated tone, he added, 'I don't know how much longer I can take it.'

By this time they were entering the station and Fox led the way up to D.I. Dormer's office on the first floor, where Rosa found herself confronted by Savill, Dormer, another officer and an alarmed-looking Toby who greeted her arrival with a look of intense relief.

'It's only a small matter before Mr Nash departs,' Savill said affably. 'I'd like to have a sample of his head hair, but he insisted you should be sent for before anything was done.'

'Is this for the lab?' Rosa asked.

'Yes.'

'Which means you've found hairs other than Tricia Langley's at the scene of the murder?'

Savill nodded. 'Got it in one, Miss Epton.'

Rosa turned to Toby. 'Go ahead and let them take a sample. You've got nothing to worry about.'

'He's also got plenty to spare,' Savill said with a cheerful smile.

At this Toby managed a sheepish grin. 'You'll probably find a few loose ones on my jacket collar,' he remarked.

'I think we'll take from source,' Savill said. 'I always like to know exactly what I'm buying and men have been known to have strange hairs clinging to their clothes.'

CHAPTER 17

About six o'clock the next evening four officers sat down in Savill's office to discuss the latest development. An extra chair had had to be fetched from a neighbouring room and Detective Sergeants Speed and Holthouse sat side by side against the wall. Inspector Dormer, as befitted his seniority, sat in the visitors' chair which was a degree less uncomfortable than the other two. It was he who spoke.

'You've got enough to charge him,' he said confidently. 'No need to look any further.'

'Hmm!' Savill replied. 'Nevertheless I'd like to have a bit more against him. Just one final piece of evidence to clinch the case.'

'You've got it, sir. The hair. The lab say that the Nash sample is identical with the hair found on the pillow and they're able to eliminate Oliver's. What more do you want?'

'Just a bit more than that,' Savill replied mildly.

Dormer looked at him in exasperation. 'I can't see what's troubling you. We've had convictions in the past on the evidence of a single fingerprint or of the debris found in trouser turn-ups. A hair is just as conclusive as that.'

Savill, however, was plainly unconvinced. 'If Nash had been our only suspect from the outset and we'd been slowly building a case against him, I wouldn't hesitate. But there are other suspects, one of whom we still haven't been able to trace. That's why I want to be as sure as possible before we arrest Nash.'

'All I can say, sir, is that if I were in charge of the enquiry, Master Nash would already be under lock and key.' Small wonder the Metropolitan Police had lost so much of its authority when you had Detective Superintendents frightened of taking decisions, he reflected savagely.

'Couldn't we just bring Nash in for a good long interrogation, sir?' Sergeant Holthouse said. 'We could always let him go if he had a satisfactory explanation for his hair being found on the dead girl's pillow.'

Savill gave a hollow laugh. 'That might work but for the fact Rosa Epton's his solicitor. I can't see her sitting back while her client is at a station helping police with their enquiries. She'd be thumping the door and demanding his immediate release.'

'Let her thump, I'd say,' Dormer remarked scornfully. 'That's about all she could do.'

'It's far from being all she could do,' Savill said quietly. 'Before we knew where we were, she'd be flying off to the High Court and applying for a writ of *habeas corpus*.'

'Who cares about that? By the time she's got her writ, you'll have charged Nash and she can stuff it.'

'And if we've not charged him or if, as things turn out, we've wrongly charged him, what then? I'll tell you. There'll be a helluva lot of answering to be done to the Commissioner, the Home Office and a pack of baying M.P.s.'

'M.P.s!' Dormer said contemptuously. 'I've never yet worried about them.'

'That may be your personal view of them, Inspector, but it's not the Commissioner's practice to thumb his nose at our legislators.'

'Of course, sir, you could always get him along here with Miss Epton,' Sergeant Holthouse said.

'And have him answer "no comment" to every question I put,' Savill observed bleakly.

'If he won't answer reasonable questions, you can use that against him,' Dormer said. 'It'll show he has something to hide.'

'Not if he's been cautioned that he needn't say anything. And I should feel obliged to caution him at an early stage.'

Dormer let out a snort. 'I know that I bloody well wouldn't. I'd shake him until his toenails dropped out and I'd got a confession.'

'Without even cautioning him?' Savill enquired with a quizzically raised eyebrow.

Dormer gave him an old-fashioned look. 'What one actually

138

does and what one subsequently tells the court one did are two different things, as every police officer knows. I'd say that I administered the caution once I'd decided to charge him. Even the smartest counsel and the most awkward judge can't unseat you if you stick to that.'

'I don't agree, but let's not argue the point further,' Savill said curtly. He glanced toward the two sergeants sitting like Tweedledum and Tweedledee. 'Inspector Dormer has given his view, now let's hear what you two have to say. Do we have enough to arrest Nash and charge him with murder or do we dig around for a bit more evidence? Peter?'

'I think we do have enough, sir,' Sergeant Holthouse said. 'It's not an overwhelming case, but we have both motive and opportunity. He wanted to make sure the girl couldn't give evidence against him and, if we accept the murder was committed between seven and seven thirty on Friday evening, Nash could have done it, as he didn't arrive at Miss Epton's flat to take her out to dinner until a quarter to eight, and it wouldn't have taken him more than fifteen minutes to drive from Fillery Street to Campden Hill.'

'If he was lucky,' Savill remarked. 'Remember it was Friday evening and the rush hour wouldn't have been over.'

'Well, he *could* have made it in fifteen minutes, sir,' Holthouse replied. 'Moreover, if he killed her closer to seven o'clock than half past, that would have given him a greater margin of time.'

'True.' Turning to Sergeant Speed, Savill said, 'What about you, Brian, what's your view?'

'I feel the same as you do, sir. It would be nice to have a bit more ... '

'Of course it would be *nice*,' Dormer broke in impatiently, 'but that's not the point. Do we already have enough and my answer's yes.'

'Go on, Brian,' Savill said, ignoring the outburst.

'And for the same reasons as you've put forward, sir,' Speed went on. 'Leaving aside the finding of Nash's hair, I'd regarded the landlord, Oliver, as the strongest suspect. He had a better opportunity than anybody else and, even if he doesn't have any

139

previous convictions, he looks just what the girls have called him, a dirty old man. In my view he bears all the marks of a sexual offender.'

'Except that he doesn't have any previous convictions,' Savill observed.

'He must have been lucky,' Speed said firmly. 'Like you, sir, I also wish we'd been able to trace Rossington, who appears to have had a motive and whose disappearance definitely calls for an explanation. It may turn out that he has an alibi, but, for the moment, he's still on my list of suspects.'

'So?'

'If we could find Rossington and eliminate him from the enquiry, that, in one sense, would strengthen the case against Nash.' He leaned forward and said earnestly, 'I'd advise holding off for another day or two, sir, while we make an all-out attempt to trace Rossington.' He paused as a puzzled frown formed on his brow.

'You look as if you're about to say something further, Brian,' Savill said, after a few seconds silence.

'I hesitate to mention it, sir, but it is something that's been puzzling me on and off ever since I visited Miss Langley's place of work. I kept on intercepting strangely furtive glances from the firm's book-keeper, Joyce Wyngard. Her behaviour was definitely odd. You could even say suspicious. And we do know that Miss Langley disliked her.'

'What are you suggesting?' Savill asked in an interested tone.

'I don't think I'm suggesting anything, sir,' Speed said lamely. 'But ... ' He gave a small resigned shrug. 'But I can't help remembering that Miss Wyngard's hair is about the same length and colour as the one found on the pillow. Sounds a bit unlikely ... '

'More than a bit unlikely, if you ask me,' Dormer broke in. 'Sounds bloody silly.'

'Thanks, Brian,' Savill said. 'Perhaps we ought to investigate Miss Wyngard as well as mount a full-scale search for Rossington.'

140

'Does that mean you're not going to arrest Nash?' Dormer asked aggressively.

Savill nodded. 'I've come to the conclusion that we're not going to lose anything by waiting a day or two longer. He's obviously not going to commit any further murders, nor do I see him fleeing the country.'

Inspector Dormer let out an angry snort. 'If that's all, I'll get back to my own station,' he said.

'Thank you for coming, Inspector. May I ask if you're proposing to continue your own enquiries into the alleged attempt to pervert the course of justice?'

'Once you've charged Nash with murder, I certainly shall, because then I'll have the leverage to crack him open and, with luck, the Epton woman as well.'

CHAPTER 18

Nell was sitting on an upturned packing case contentedly suckling her baby while Max, considerably less contentedly, was endeavouring to install their recently acquired third-hand washing machine in the adjoining room. The room in which Nell sat was bare apart from the packing case and two mattresses, plus a valise and a duffel bag from which various items of clothing spilled.

Max was the father of the baby, though not Nell's husband, and the scene of this domestic activity was a Squat in North London. It was the end house of a terrace which was awaiting demolition.

Nell and Max and the baby had moved in six weeks earlier after joining the ranks of London's young homeless. A number of other couples, some with, some without children, also occupied rooms in the house. At the moment, however, everybody else was out.

A young man known as Jimp had lived there until a week before, but had then suddenly left without a word to anyone. He was regarded as being a bit strange in the head, and generally unco-operative, so that his abrupt departure had gone unmourned, even in their live-and-let-live society. Somebody had moved into his room within a day or two, though nobody had seen very much of him as yet.

'Have you seen Peter the last day or so?' Nell called out through the open door as she offered her baby the other teat.

'What?' Max shouted back through an onslaught of hammering.

'Peter, have you seen him recently?'

'Who's Peter?'

'Peter, the chap who took over Jimp's room.'

'Oh, him!'

142

'Well, have you?'

'Have I what?'

'Seen him? Because I haven't.'

They often held these long-distance conversations which Nell rather enjoyed. She had a serene nature and seldom showed impatience or irritability.

'Nor have I,' Max replied.

'Do you think he's all right?'

'How should I know. Anyway, why shouldn't he be all right?'

'I think I'll go up and see when I've fed Tom.' No response came apart from some further hammering and she went on, 'He could be lying dead up there without anyone knowing.'

'We'd have smelt something.'

'Not in this house in January we wouldn't. Jimp didn't have any heating at all. Anyway, what I really meant was that he may be ill.'

'He could call out.'

'Not if he's lost his voice,' Nell remarked, with her own brand of logic.

'Then he could bang on the floor.'

'He may be too weak. And even if he did, we wouldn't necessarily hear two floors below.'

'Why can't he just have gone out?'

'Because I haven't seen him go out, that's why.'

Max was either pondering this or giving all his attention to the washing machine for half a minute passed before he spoke again.

'You didn't always see Jimp come and go.'

'That was because he kept such curious hours.'

'So may this Peter chap.'

'Anyway, there's no harm in my going up to see.'

'If he is up there and not dead or dying, you might ask him to come down and give me a hand with this flaming machine.'

'Can't you fix it?'

'There are pieces missing,' he said savagely.

Nell got up from the packing case and gently laid her baby

143

in the carry-cot which Max had made out of an old deck-chair and some curtain rods. She then carried Tom into the next room where she found the floor littered with what she assumed to be bits of washing machine. She put the carry-cot down on one of the few clear spaces.

'Keep an eye on Tom,' she said, 'and I'll just run upstairs.'

The room to which she made her way was at the very top of the house and was the only singly-occupied one in the Squat. It was about large enough to take a narrow bed and no more and was, in fact, a hived off slice of the attic. The final approach to the top floor was up a narrow box staircase.

Nell had only been up there a couple of times before and had found it distinctly spooky with sinister noises coming from the water tank.

She arrived out of breath after the steep climb and knocked on the door. She somehow didn't expect a reply and none came. She knew that the door couldn't be locked as there were no locks on any of them. Indeed, in their easy-going communal life, it was rare for anyone even to trouble to close a door.

She turned the handle and pushed the door open. There was a stale, tangy smell and she saw Peter lying on his side with his face to the wall. His legs were drawn up and only the top of his head was visible. His overcoat lay spread over the two old army blankets which Jimp had left behind. The room was icily cold.

'Are you all right, Peter?' she asked softly.

She moved a step closer to the bed and touched his shoulder.

'It's Nell. I came to see if you needed anything.'

Even as she spoke, she recognised the futility of her words, for she really had little doubt that Peter was dead. She pulled back the overcoat and blankets sufficiently to see his face and noticed a patch of dried vomit beside his head.

Stretching out a hand, she touched his forehead, which was as cold as the room itself. Satisfied that he was beyond her ministrations, she returned downstairs.

'He's dead,' she said to Max who was still on his knees wrestling with the washing machine.

'Dead?' he said, without looking up.

'Peter. In Jimp's old room. I've just been up there.'

When he was absorbed in something else, Max never listened to what she said, so that she was quite used to repeating herself. Anyone but Nell would have been driven mad by him on such occasions, but she remained serenely patient.

'Good God!' he exclaimed, now staring at her in disbelief. 'Are you sure?'

She nodded. 'What do you think we'd better do?'

'I'll go and take a look for myself. You come, too.'

She glanced down at Tom who was sleeping peacefully in his makeshift cot. Her first concern was always that *he* had nothing to complain about.

She followed Max up to the top of the house and stood just behind him as he made his own inspection of the room.

'It looks to me as if he took an overdose,' he remarked, stepping over to the window and picking up a small plastic phial to read its label. 'Empty. I wonder how many he took?'

'Poor Peter, I wonder why he did it,' Nell said, sadly.

Max gave a small grunt and stooped down to pick up a folded sheet of paper off the floor where it appeared to have fallen from the narrow window sill.

'Maybe this'll tell us.'

He read it in silence and then handed it to Nell without comment.

The note read:

I apologise to everyone at the Squat who has been so kind to me since I arrived. I trust my departure won't cause anyone too much inconvenience. I've decided, however, to end my life in the hope of joining Tricia on the other side where I know we'll both be happier than we have been in this creation. I know the police want to interview me about her death, but I have no wish to talk to them. That's all – except goodbye. Peter Rossington.

'I wonder who Tricia was?' Nell said in a thoughtful voice.

'Probably his wife or his girl-friend,' Max replied. 'Wonder how she died.'

Nobody at the Squat, apart from Peter, ever read a

145

newspaper save on a Sunday, when they would share a copy of *The Observer*. In any event, it's doubtful if the news of Tricia's murder, tucked away on an inside page, would have attracted anyone's notice.

'What are we going to do?' Nell asked, handing back the note.

'For a start, we can't just leave him here.'

'We'll have to tell somebody.'

Max nodded. 'It's not as if we could get an ambulance to take him off to hospital. And we can't dispose of him ourselves, though I'm sure he wouldn't mind if we could. It looks as if we'll have to inform the police, which is an invitation to a lot of aggro.'

'Why don't we wait until everyone's back this evening and we can discuss it?'

'What's the time now?'

'One thirty.'

'Nobody'll be back before five.'

'The police needn't know we discovered him now.'

Max stood staring out of the small dirty window with its cracked pane of glass, a heavy frown on his face.

'But what are the alternatives?' he said at last. 'We've agreed we can't just leave him up here to moulder.'

'Wouldn't an undertaker remove him?'

'Not before a doctor had signed a death certificate. And no doctor is going to do that without reporting his findings to the coroner. I'm afraid I can't see any alternative to notifying the police. And in that case, the sooner it's done, the better. Perhaps they won't cause too much aggro after all. There's precious little any of us can tell them.' He glanced down at the suicide note in his hand. 'I didn't even know his name was Rossington.'

And so to their combined relief, it proved to be. By the time the others returned, the body had already been taken away and as they all sat down to supper that evening, eager to speculate about the dramatic happening, a car pulled up outside and out got Detective Superintendent Savill and Detective Sergeant Speed.

More than one member of the Squat had had past brushes

with the forces of law and order, but even they grudgingly admitted later that the two officers had behaved in as reasonable and civilised a fashion as could be expected of the police.

It didn't take Savill long to establish that Peter Rossington had been there a week, having been befriended by Martin and Ruth who had found him in a pub drinking as though all the sorrows of the world were pressing on his shoulders. They had brought him back that evening and introduced him to the others. Thereafter, however, nobody had seen much of him and it was clear that he preferred to be on his own at the top of the house. He would often slip out for an hour or two in the middle of the day and return with a newspaper (this information came from Nell), but for the past two days he hadn't been seen at all.

'Didn't he even come down and have his evening meal with the rest of you?' Savill had asked.

A chorus of voices informed him that this only happened on the first evening and thereafter he had returned from his expeditions with take-away food from the local Kebab Restaurant.

The one detail of which they were all certain was that it had been the previous Friday he had joined the Squat. Martin and Ruth had come across him in the pub around nine thirty that evening. He was dejected and morose but, despite Ruth's subtle probing, had given no reason for his obvious deep unhappiness.

When Savill told them who Tricia was, they became agog with interest. After his departure – and for the next few evenings – there was no other topic of conversation.

As Savill and Speed drove away from the house, Speed said, 'I wonder how long he'd been dead, sir?'

'The pathologist should give us an idea of that soon enough. What interests me is that he moved in there on the evening of Tricia Langley's murder.'

Speed nodded. 'What do you make of the suicide note, sir?'

'It can be interpreted either way. As an oblique confession of murder or not.'

'If he had murdered her, I'd have expected him to say so.'

'Not necessarily,' Savill said. 'Murderers, particularly those with a sensitive conscience, often take refuge in evasion. He may have reasoned that an outright confession would have spoilt his chances of joining her in the hereafter, as seems to have been his hope.'

'He must have been a nut if he expected that,' Speed observed.

'I wouldn't know,' Savill said. 'At the moment, my interest is in the here and now. In particular what forensic will tell us about Rossington's hair sample we'll be sending them.'

Savill had the answer to this the next day when the laboratory informed him that it bore no resemblance whatever to the one found on Tricia's pillow. By then it had also been confirmed that Peter had died of barbiturate poisoning as a result of a massive overdose of sleeping tablets.

Since the discovery of his body, intensive efforts had been made to trace his movements in the hours that preceded his arrival at the pub where Martin and Ruth had met him. Savill was not, however, particularly hopeful that these would be successful. He was especially anxious to find out where Peter had been between seven and eight on that Friday evening.

He found himself silently cursing Peter for having left, as his farewell to life, a note couched in such ambiguous language. Why couldn't he have said plainly whether or not he killed Tricia? If he had made a confession of murder, it could have been accepted as true. If he had explicitly denied it, it might have been true or it might not, though Savill would have been inclined to believe it. In his experience, suicides usually left notes which were truthful as far as they went. They might not represent the whole truth, but they rarely contained mischief-making falsehoods.

As for D.I. Dormer, he remained as uncompromising in his views as ever. As soon as he heard the news of Peter Rossington's suicide, he phoned Savill to learn the details.

'I never did think it was him,' he said bluntly when Savill had brought him up to date on events. He went on, 'I recall your saying at our last con that you'd feel more confident about charging Nash once Rossington had been eliminated as a suspect. As I see it, he has been.'

'Certainly the hair on the pillow didn't come from him,' Savill conceded.

'If he'd done it, he'd have said so in the note he left.'

'But why did he go to ground after her death and end up living anonymously in a North London Squat?'

'Because he was a neurotic young man. He was upset by her death and decided to end his own life. If he had murdered her, he'd have done himself in at the same time. He was that type. We'd have found both of them dead in her room.'

Savill had already thought of this and considered it a sound point. It meant, however, it could have been no more than a coincidence that Martin and Ruth met him drinking away his sorrows on the very evening of Tricia's death. It also meant that his almost incoherent phone call to the flat on Sunday evening had been made without knowledge of her death. This he must have learnt from the papers a day or so later. As, according to the pathologist, he had been dead for at least two days before discovery of his body, he must have killed himself shortly after learning the news.

All this passed through Savill's mind again as he talked to D.I. Dormer. It was a perfectly logical explanation of events and the more he thought about it, the more plausible it seemed.

Dormer now broke in on his thoughts. 'I take it you don't seriously suspect the woman in Tricia Langley's office?'

'Sergeant Speed went to see her yesterday. She told him that the girl disliked her because she, Miss Wyngard, had rebuked her for bad time-keeping and for not showing a responsible attitude to her work.'

'Well, that obviously lets her out. Not that I ever considered her in. But she wouldn't have committed murder for such a paltry reason as a bit of office huff.'

'Speed still felt she was hiding something. He also formed the opinion that she'd have been quite capable physically of doing it.'

149

Dormer gave an impatient snort. 'Did he get round to asking her where she was on that Friday evening?'

'Yes. She was alone at home. She has a flat near Hurlingham Club, not very far from Fillery Street.'

'Did he also ask her for a sample of her hair?' Dormer enquired with a faint sneer.

'He didn't feel he had enough on her to justify that, but he took a loose one from her chair when she wasn't looking. Unfortunately it turned out to come from the cat.'

Dormer let out a harsh laugh. Serve the idiot right, it clearly said.

'In my view, you have only two suspects left. Oliver, the landlord, and Nash. And everything points to Nash. He's the one with both opportunity and an eighteen carat motive. If Oliver's the sex maniac you've all been suggesting, how come he'd not made a pass at her before. She was often alone at the flat at weekends, so why'd he wait till that particular weekend?'

'There always has to be a first time,' Savill replied. 'Obviously I can't tell you why he hadn't tried anything before. Perhaps he felt particularly lustful that weekend. Perhaps he'd been thinking about it for months, but had managed to restrain himself. After all, why does a man choose one moment rather than another to stick a knife into his nagging wife? He could do it any day out of three hundred and sixty five in the year, but eventually a moment comes.'

'But it wasn't his hair found on the pillow,' Dormer said, brushing aside Savill's analogy.

'I'm aware of that.'

'In my view, you're taking a big risk leaving Master Nash to run around free.'

'At times, you sound really vindictive toward Nash,' Savill said, stung by the other's persistence and by the feeling of being hustled into action which he still wished to consider.

'I don't like seeing criminals flouting the law and getting away with it,' Dormer said stonily.

After he had rung off, Savill realised that, were it not for Dormer's blatant antagonism toward Toby Nash, he might have fewer doubts about arresting him. Though Nash had had opportunity, he was still unhappy about the motive. Admittedly, if one accepted that it was the only way of silencing Tricia, then Toby Nash had a very strong motive. But had that really been the situation? It seemed to Savill that the defence wouldn't have much difficulty in destroying it. They would be able to show that she had been a most reluctant witness who had, so to speak, been saved only by the bell on her appearance in the witness box.

If only he could get Nash to the station without his solicitor, he could give him a proper grilling. He could keep him there twenty-four hours on the time-honoured pretext that he was helping police with their enquiries. After that he would either have to be charged or allowed to go.

A thoughtful expression formed on his face. Perhaps there was a possibility of engineering it. The weekend had begun. Supposing Rosa Epton had gone away, but Toby Nash had not ... In those circumstances he might be able to get something out of Nash, before Rosa could come galloping to his aid. It seemed a possibility worth exploring.

Every officer will admit that he needs a slice of luck in a difficult investigation and Savill felt that such had come his way when, by use of guile, he discovered that Rosa was, indeed, out of town for the weekend, having hurried off to visit her father who had had a bad fall.

So it came about that, instead of spending Saturday evening drinking with friends in a pub, Toby found himself at the police station in circumstances that were anything but friendly.

CHAPTER 19

Rosa had received a telephone call about her father around nine o'clock on Friday evening and had set off immediately.

Mrs Williams, who was one of her father's faithful parishioners, had sounded breathless and agitated on the telephone. She told Rosa that her father had slipped and fallen in the kitchen and then lain unconscious until Marion, one of the lodgers from the agricultural college, found him lying on the floor. The doctor had been and had advised that he should be removed to hospital for a more detailed examination.

Before leaving home, Rosa phoned Robin Snaith to tell him what had happened, adding that she hoped to be back in the office on Monday morning, but would keep in touch with him. She also tried to call Toby, but could get no reply. In any event, she was confident that nothing was likely to happen over the weekend.

She arrived at the rectory some time after midnight to find a note from Mrs Williams awaiting her on the hall table, saying that her father was comfortable, that x-rays had failed to reveal any fractures and that he was likely to be discharged from hospital within a day or two. A postscript informed her that the Reverend Birkenshaw would take all services on Sunday and a further postscript added that the Reverend B. was Mrs Young's nephew and happened to be staying with his aunt for a few days.

There was a second note on the table. This was from Marion, the agricultural student. It read:

Gather you'll be arriving late. Gather you have key. Gather your father will be O.K. See you in morning, I expect. Marion.

The next day, Saturday, Mrs Williams arrived about eight o'clock, just as Rosa was making herself some tea and toast.

'I'm so glad you're here, dear. I hope I didn't sound alarmist on the telephone, but one never knows, does one?'

Rosa agreed, without being too sure what about.

When later that morning she drove over to the hospital, she found her father sitting up in bed doing *The Times* crossword.

'Good heavens, what are you doing here?' he said in a tone of the utmost surprise.

'Mrs Williams phoned me last night and told me what had happened.'

He shook his head in mild dismay. 'Oh dear, I do wish she didn't enjoy creating dramas so much. Not that it isn't delightful seeing you, Rosa.' He paused. 'But do you mean you drove all the way from London last night?'

'Yes. I arrived soon after midnight.'

'My poor child, you must be tired out.'

'No, I'm not and, anyway, it was worth the journey to find you looking so perky. Now I know you're all right, I'll go back after lunch tomorrow. How did you come to fall?'

'I'd been out in the garden and picked up a wet leaf on the heel of my shoe. I don't really remember much more until I was in the ambulance.'

'How long was it before Marion found you?'

'I think she arrived back a few minutes afterwards.'

'Mrs Williams made it sound as if you'd lain unconscious on the kitchen floor for hours.'

'Nonsense. Five minutes at the most.'

Rosa paid him a second visit in the early evening, but spent the rest of the day reading and going for a long walk. She had always loved the austereness of the winter countryside and today it seemed to reflect her mood more than ever.

On Sunday morning she visited her father again and found him further improved.

'Are you sure you're not working too hard?' he asked suddenly, giving her a worried look.

'No harder than usual. And, anyway, I enjoy having lots of work.'

'You look pale,' he said, 'and your eyes are not shining the

153

way they usually do. Are you sure you're not feeling the strain?'

'I have got a rather tricky case at the moment,' she said, 'but it'll all come right. There's nothing to worry about.'

He continued, however, to look at her with an anxious expression. 'I wish I could help you in some way, but I don't suppose I can.'

'I promise you I'm all right,' she replied stoutly. 'One has these phases of intense work, but they never last for ever.'

'As long as it's only work and not a personal problem that's troubling you.'

'Now, stop worrying about me, daddy! I'm all right. Make sure you get the same way!'

It was with a certain relief that she kissed him goodbye and returned to the rectory, where she found another of Marion's notes on the hall table. This one read:

Have gone out. Sam Brazier phoned. Wants you to call him as soon as you return. Marion. P.S. If you've left before I get back, ta-ta

There could only be one reason for Sam ringing her in the depths of Herefordshire on a Sunday morning. Toby.

As she dialled his number, she felt thankful that she was all alone in the house and there was nobody to overhear her conversation. She gave a small shiver at the thought of her father ever learning of her involvement with Toby. His fall in the kitchen would pale into insignificance compared with the shock that would give him.

'It's Rosa,' she said as soon as she heard Sam's voice on the other end of the line. 'What's happened to Toby?'

'He's been arrested.'

'Arrested?'

'Well, taken away by the police.'

'When did this happen?'

'Yesterday evening. I found a scrawled note from him when I got home in the early hours of this morning. I'd been to a party near Chelmsford,' he added by way of explaining his late return. 'I rang around until I got through to the right police station and they confirmed he was there.'

'Did you speak to Superintendent Savill or one of his officers?'

'I don't know who I spoke to. I was put through to the C.I.D. and a voice merely said he was helping them with enquiries and then rang off.'

'I wish you'd called me immediately.'

'I tried your flat, but there was no reply and I had to wait until this morning to find out where you were.'

'Yes, of course, I'm sorry. I came down here in a great hurry. My father had been taken off to hospital.'

'How is he?'

'Much better.'

'Good. Is there anything you want me to do about Toby?'

'I don't think so. I was about to set off for home in an hour or so, but I'll come now and go straight to the station when I reach town. Will you be in this evening?'

'I can be. I usually go out for a quiet drink on Sunday evenings, but I'll stay in if you want me to.'

'I'll call you and let you know developments. Incidentally, are you sure the person you spoke to at the station used the expression "helping us with enquiries"?'

'Certain.'

'Then it looks as if he wasn't arrested. They've hauled him in for questioning in the hope he'll make some damaging admission which'll enable them to charge him. What did he actually say in the note he left you?'

'It was a bit melodramatic. I've not got it here at the moment. He said he was being kidnapped by the police and I must find you and let you know what had happened.' Sam paused before adding, 'The police must be mad if they believe Toby murdered Tricia.'

'Mad or perverted,' Rosa observed grimly. 'Anyway, the sooner I get to the station, the better.'

It was around half past four that afternoon when Rosa arrived back and parked in a side street close to the police station.

By then Toby had been there just over twenty hours. Twenty hours during which, apart from a small number of breaks for

155

refreshment and a few hours of sleep, he had been pounded with questions. Questions which had sometimes been cajoling and friendly and sometimes threatening, but more often somewhere in between those extremes.

It seemed to Rosa that she was half-expected, for when she announced herself to the uniformed officer on front desk duty, he just gave a nod and asked her to wait a minute. He then disappeared, to return a few minutes later accompanied by Detective Superintendent Savill.

Savill's hair was rumpled, his eyes red-rimmed and his shirt collar button undone. He might have been a reporter who had been up all night on a story – or a police officer who had been trying to wring a confession out of a suspect.

'Good afternoon, Miss Epton. I thought you might turn up.'

'I want to know what my client is doing here.'

'Helping us with enquiries,' he said with a small deprecating smile.

'So he's not under arrest?'

'Is that what you were expecting, Miss Epton?'

'I merely want to ascertain his status. If he's been charged, I wish to see him immediately. If he hasn't been, I shall advise him to leave. You have no right to hold him.'

'Hold him, Miss Epton?' Savill said as though mystified by her meaning. 'He came here voluntarily to help us.'

'Don't insult my intelligence!' she said angrily. In a calmer tone she added, 'But if he came here voluntarily, he can just as easily leave voluntarily. I'll be glad, therefore, if you'll now let me see him so that I may advise him of his rights.'

Savill studied her in silence for a minute as though trying to make up his mind what to do.

'The hair found on Miss Langley's pillow is identical with the hairs in the sample provided by Nash,' he said matter-of-factly, while continuing to watch her.

Rosa drew in her breath sharply. 'Go on,' she said in a brittle voice.

'It's pretty damning evidence against him, isn't it?'

'If you think so, why haven't you charged him?'

156

'I wanted to give him every chance of explaining it.'

'Twenty hours seems long enough.'

'The trouble has been that he can't explain its presence. Not satisfactorily, that is.'

'What you really mean is that you've been unable to get him to confess to a crime he didn't commit.'

'How are you to know whether he committed it or not, Miss Epton?' he asked, in a gently mocking tone.

Rosa felt herself blushing. 'He's told me he didn't murder her,' she said stoutly.

'And you believe everything a client tells you?' Savill asked in the same tone as before.

'In this instance, yes.'

'Your client strikes me as a very plausible young man. A bit too plausible perhaps.'

'I'm really not very interested in your views on him,' Rosa said loftily. 'I'd like to see him please. Now.'

Savill got up from his chair. 'As a matter of fact,' he said, 'I was about to have him charged when you arrived. But I thought it'd be courteous to speak to you first. Shall we now go up to my office?'

Rosa licked her lips that had gone suddenly dry. 'You're going to charge him with Tricia Langley's murder?'

'That's right.'

'Then you'll be making a terrible mistake,' she said vehemently.

'That'll be for a jury to say.'

She shook her head. 'No, it won't. *I'm* going to prove it to you.'

CHAPTER 20

Toby's appearance the next morning before the stipendiary magistrate at Fulham Court was brief. Detective Superintendent Savill asked for a week's remand in custody and Rosa applied for legal aid, both applications being granted. She had warned Toby in advance that he stood no chance at that stage of getting bail on a murder charge.

As soon as the hearing was over, she made her way to the cells where he greeted her with a wan smile.

'I suppose it's back to Brixton prison?' he said.

'I'm afraid so.'

'If it weren't so bloody serious, I'd feel like laughing. It must be the craziest charge the police have ever brought. You don't believe I murdered Tricia, do you?'

'I'm quite certain you didn't,' Rosa replied promptly. 'What's more, that's the very first time I've ever answered that question from a client. Usually, I tell them it's not part of my job to believe in their innocence, so my view is irrelevant.'

He seemed not to hear her. 'Did I look like somebody who'd just committed a murder when I picked you up for dinner that Friday evening?' he asked in a disbelieving voice.

'Of course you didn't.'

'I swear I never entered her flat again after New Year's Eve. I suppose I must have shed one of my hairs on that occasion and fate waited to drop it later on her pillow.'

Rosa said nothing. Her own theory didn't embrace the possibility of fate having played any part at all. But she didn't wish to voice her suspicions to Toby at that juncture.

'I'll come and see you in a couple of days,' she said. 'Meanwhile I promise you I shan't be idle. In fact,' she went on as if talking aloud to herself, 'I shan't rest until a monstrous injustice has been put right. If the police are no longer interested

158

in who really murdered Tricia, I shall have to force them to become interested again.'

Toby gazed at her with a degree of awe. He had never seen her in such a grimly determined mood. It was clear that an iron will lurked behind that elfin face. He gave her one of his boyish smiles to break the spell she seemed to have cast over both of them.

'At least, we'll now have something further to celebrate when I'm free again.'

'You'll be free all right, I'll see to that,' she said fiercely.

It was hard to realise that this small ferocious Boadicea was the same warm, sexually exciting girl in whose bed he had spent a night.

After she had gone, he stretched out on the wooden bench in his cell and stared at the ceiling. Even though charged with an even more serious offence than previously, he felt far less scared. He was completely confident that Rosa would get him off. He had experienced a fair number of ups and downs during the first decade of his adult life and had accepted each as it came. He'd always abhorred the thought of a routine existence and he despised security as an ideal. He had been ready to throw up his job at the bank before all this happened and it now seemed as if fate had taken a hand. He found himself sinking into an almost mellow mood as he lay on the hard wooden bench and contemplated his future.

Meanwhile, as Rosa left the building, she observed Savill, Dormer and Speed driving away together from the court. She had not noticed Dormer in court, but had no doubt he'd have been wearing a look of self-satisfied triumph.

When she got back to the office, she was relieved to find that Robin had also returned from his court engagement. She had spoken to him briefly on the telephone the previous evening and had told him what had greeted her when she arrived back from visiting her father.

He gave her a look of concern as she came in and threw herself down in his visitors' chair.

'You look worn out,' he remarked. 'If you go on like this, you'll crack up.'

159

'No, I shan't. I'm not as frail as I appear.'

Robin let out a laugh. 'I've never dreamt of calling you frail. You're much tougher than I am in many ways, but that doesn't mean you can drive yourself without any sort of let-up. And the fact you're emotionally involved with Toby Nash doesn't help.'

'My emotions are now strictly under control in that area,' she said crisply. 'But it's a dastardly thing the police have done and I'm going to prove it.'

'From what you told me on the phone last night, his hair on the dead girl's pillow was the clinching piece of evidence.'

'That's what they'll say.'

'Well, isn't it?'

'It would be if he had dropped it there, but he didn't. He couldn't have.' She fixed Robin with a concentrated look. 'It's my certain belief it was planted there to incriminate him and I'm going to prove it.'

'Planted by whom?' Robin asked in a shaken voice, though he knew what answer to expect.

'Detective Inspector Dormer, of course.'

He was silent for a while and when he spoke it was in a serious voice.

'I know you don't like Dormer – and neither do I for that matter – but do you realise the full import of what you've just said? Are you really alleging that a detective inspector planted one of Nash's hairs at the scene of the murder in order to incriminate him?'

'That's precisely what I believe happened. It's the old story, he was sure in his own mind that Toby did it and he was determined to make certain there was enough evidence against him. Mind you, put that way, it's giving Dormer the benefit of a doubt. In my view, he'd be capable of framing Toby, anyway. He's shown himself to be malicious and vindictive and frankly I wouldn't put anything past him.'

'It's a fantastic allegation.'

'I'm going to prove it.'

'When would he have made the plant?' Robin asked suspiciously.

'Sunday evening when he visited Fillery Street and discovered Tricia dead. It was a heaven sent opportunity.'

'That must mean he was carrying one of Toby Nash's hairs around in his pocket waiting for the right moment to plant it.'

'Yes.'

'That really does sound far-fetched.'

'Look at it this way. He has an appointment to see Tricia on Sunday evening. He's obviously going there to twist her arm once again about giving evidence against Toby. At the same time he'll be sure to ask her if Toby had tried to get in touch with her in breach of his bail undertaking. Being the mixed-up girl she was, she could well have said yes. In any event, he would have been ready to pressurise her with threats into saying it. Either way, the finding of one of Toby's hairs in the flat would not only support her story, but would make it more certain that she stuck to it. Then having squeezed an admission out of her, he would purport to find a hair which, he'd have told her, looks very much like one of Nash's. He'd have immediately gone off to court and asked for Toby's bail to be revoked. At the next hearing when Toby would deny having breached his undertaking, Dormer would stand up and say he had almost certain proof that he had done so. Let Toby provide a hair sample and he *could* prove it. Knowing all the time, of course, that he could, as it was one of Toby's hairs which he had carefully taken with him and allegedly found at the flat.' She paused. 'But all that became hypothetical when he arrived and found Tricia dead.'

'Where would he have got a hair from in the first place?'

'No problem over that. Most men shed hairs. Look at your own collar, Robin! And Toby had been in the police cells at Petersham on two occasions.'

Robin Snaith drew a deep breath.

'And how are you going to set about proving all this, my little Rosa?' he asked, looking at her over the top of his spectacles.

'By discovering who did murder Tricia Langley.'

'Any ideas on that?'

'It could have been Peter Rossington. He appears to have left a very strange note behind, which could easily be interpreted

161

as coming from Tricia's murderer. On the other hand, her two flat-mates believe it was their landlord.'

Robin shook his head in a gesture of doubt.

'I can't see you getting anywhere.'

'I've got to,' Rosa said in a tone that brooked no answer.

She spent that afternoon dealing with other work. She was conscious that, even though he had said nothing, Robin regarded Toby as just one more client and she had no intention of incurring even an unvoiced criticism that she was neglecting others whose cases she was handling. She was also well aware that there was no chance whatsoever of her being reimbursed for every hour she devoted to Toby's defence. A great deal of unpaid and unproductive work would be involved, so it behove her to undertake as much of it as she could in non-office hours. That was only fair to the firm in which, after all, she was junior partner.

Accordingly, when at half past five Robin put his head round her door and said he was going home and what about her? she replied that she had a brief to counsel to complete and was then off to pursue her enquiries on Toby's behalf. Robin seemed to wrestle in his mind about how to respond. In the end he said, with a small resigned smile, 'Good luck and take care.'

When Rosa stepped from her car outside 52 Fillery Street, she noticed the landlord observing her surreptitiously from his vantage point in the basement. She felt his eyes following her as she walked up the four steps to the front door. She pressed the bell of Flat 4 and a few seconds later a wary voice came through the intercom.

'It's Rosa Epton. May I come up?'

'Yes, I'll press the buzzer.'

When she reached the top of the stairs, Sara greeted her from the open flat door.

'Sorry if I sounded horribly suspicious,' she said, 'but we've had so many odd people trying to inveigle their way in. Apart from the press, there've been applicants for Tricia's room even though it's never been advertised as vacant and a number of

162

rather sinister types who seem to think we run some sort of Chamber of Horrors up here.'

'How very disagreeable,' Rosa remarked, sympathetically.

As she entered the flat, Janice emerged from the bathroom. Her face lit up when she saw Rosa.

'You're the first welcome visitor we've had for a week.'

'There was nothing wrong with Joe,' Sara said defensively.

'I wasn't counting boy-friends. They're always all right. Well, most of them. Even poor, pained Peter Rossington was normal compared with some of the people we've had ringing the bell.'

'Did you know he'd committed suicide?'

'Yes, I saw a tiny paragraph in an evening paper. Does that mean he killed Tricia?'

'Not in the police view. They've arrested and charged Toby.'

Janice gave a gasp as they both looked at Rosa in stunned amazement. Janice was the first to speak.

'But that's crazy. Toby wouldn't have murdered her in a hundred years. He wouldn't murder anyone. How on earth have the police worked that out?'

'They found one of his hairs on Tricia's pillow, which, in their view, clinched the case,' Rosa replied.

Janice frowned. 'The flat's full of male hairs,' she said. 'Half the young men we know suffer from dreaded dandruff and falling hair.' She glanced about her as if to point out a few specimens.

'On the assumption that Toby didn't murder her, how do you account for his hair being found on the pillow?'

'Somebody must have put it there,' Sara said promptly.

Before Rosa could say that was also her view, Janice began speaking in a slow, thoughtful tone.

'It must have been nosy Norm. As you know, I've always suspected him.'

'But how would he have known it was one of Toby's hairs he was putting there?' Sara broke in.

'He wouldn't have known. It was pure chance.' With growing excitement, she went on, 'Don't you see! After killing Tricia, his

163

first thought was to deflect suspicion away from himself, so he picks up a loose hair from the sofa or one of these chairs and plants it on the pillow.'

'But it might have been one of ours,' Sara expostulated.

'I don't shed mine,' Janice retorted, 'and your hair's auburn and a quite distinctive colour. All he had to do was avoid picking up one of yours or one of his own. Apart from those two, he could make his choice from a doubtless wide selection. After all, it wouldn't matter whose it was, it would still serve to send the police off on a false trail. It was pure chance and rotten luck for Toby that it happened to be one of his.'

Rosa had listened attentively to Janice's persuasively propounded theory. Even though it didn't match her own, it would be premature to dismiss it.

'Has your landlord been keeping out of your way recently?' she asked.

Janice gave a mirthless laugh. 'No such luck. He pounces on me at every opportunity. We also suspect he comes up to the flat when we're out. There've been tell-tale signs.'

'Why should he do that?' Rosa asked curiously.

'He's a born snooper in addition to all his other loathsome habits. We know he was up here this morning as he told us so when we arrived back this evening. Apparently the police wanted to make another search of Tricia's room and he let them into the flat.'

'I think the moment has come when I must have a word with him,' Rosa remarked in a thoughtful tone.

'You're welcome to him.'

'And you still believe he killed Tricia?'

'More than ever,' Janice said emphatically. 'He's a hundred times more likely murderer than Toby. No, a thousand times.'

Rosa pondered this in silence for a while, then she said, 'I'd like to talk to Miss Greenwood. Would this be a good moment to visit her?'

Janice shook her head. 'She'll be out. A friend takes her off to her home for supper every Monday evening. She'll be back about nine thirty.'

'I'll leave it till tomorrow. I can ring her and find out when it'll be convenient to come.'

'Are you going to call on Norm this evening?' Sara asked.

'Yes. I'll go down and see him now.'

The two girls accompanied her to the front door where they exchanged friendly goodbyes.

'Give Toby my love when you see him,' Janice said. 'If he's allowed visitors tell him I'll trek down to Brixton at the weekend. Prison visiting will be a new experience.'

From the slightly apprehensive look she cast her friend, Sara apparently felt that it might be compromising to send *her* love to someone charged with murder.

As Rosa made her way downstairs, she realised what an effective early warning system nosy Norm had. There was scarcely one stair that didn't react in noisy protest when trodden on. She closed the house door behind her and glanced down into the basement area in time to glimpse the twitch of a curtain. Although he must have heard her further descent to his own door, it was a full minute before he answered the bell.

'Good evening, Mr Oliver,' Rosa said. 'We haven't met before, but my name's Rosa Epton and I'm a solicitor. May I come in?'

Whatever other appetites were gnawing away at the land-lord's gut, curiosity was without doubt the strongest.

'Yes, of course,' he said in a welcoming tone. 'You've been visiting the girls, haven't you? I happened to be looking out of the window when you arrived.' He ushered her into his living-room and indicated a chair in the manner of a fussy major-domo before sitting down opposite her. 'I think you said you were a solicitor?'

'That's right. I'm representing Toby Nash.' She paused to observe his reaction to the name, but he merely assumed an expression of polite interest. 'Do you know who I mean, Mr Oliver?'

'Toby Nash?' he said slowly. 'No, I don't think I've ever met him.'

'You've not read one of this evening's papers?'

His expression became instantly wary. 'I'm afraid not. Was there something about him?'

'He's been arrested and charged with the murder of Tricia Langley.'

Norman started as if he had received a vicious kick on the ankle.

'No, no, I know nothing about that. But what a relief that the police have caught the man!' He took out a handkerchief and blew his nose loudly. 'You must excuse me, Miss Epton,' he went on, dabbing at his eyes. 'Of course I never doubted they would, but it's been a tremendous strain for all of us here. I'm sure the girls must feel as relieved as I am by the news. They're really wonderful, our police, aren't they? The envy of every country in the world. And rightly so. There isn't a situation they can't handle. It's the same with our system of justice. There isn't another to touch it. I'm sorry, what must you think of me prattling on like this?' Fortunately no answer was expected, though Rosa did reflect that both the police and the system of justice deserved a less dubious propagandist. 'I must pull myself together, but your news has really taken me by surprise. You were mentioning that you represented the person charged with this terrible crime. Toby Nash, you said. I'm sure I've never met him.'

'You may know him by sight. He visited Tricia here on a few occasions.'

Norman gave an indulgent laugh. 'So many young men beat tracks to that top flat. But what can one expect when it houses such attractive girls?'

'Tricia was particularly attractive,' Rosa remarked tendentiously.

'Oh, yes. Enormously attractive. I often used to wish I was twenty years younger.' He suddenly paused and frowned. 'But you knew her, did you?'

'Yes. I defended Nash when he was charged with raping her.'

Norman's hand flew up to his mouth, as though to shut off the escape of any further confidences.

'Oh, my God!' he gasped. 'It's *that* young man is it?'

'Maybe you have met him after all?'

'No, never. And I'm not at all sure I ought to be talking to you,' he said in an agitated voice.

'There's absolutely no reason why you shouldn't be. You're not yet a prosecution witness and may never become one.'

'I don't think Superintendent Savill would approve.'

'There's no need to tell him.'

'Oh dear, oh dear, oh dear, what an awkward business!'

'Concentrate on your feeling of relief that an arrest has been made,' Rosa said drily. She felt like adding, and that it isn't you. 'As a matter of fact, Mr Oliver, there's only one matter on which I'd be glad of your help. On the Sunday evening that Tricia's body was discovered, I understand you accompanied the officer, Detective Inspector Dormer, up to the flat and unlocked the door for him. Is that right?'

'Yes. It was my duty as landlord and as a responsible citizen to allow him access.'

'Of course. I'm not criticising you. All I'd like to know is exactly what happened when you got inside?'

Norman didn't have many opportunities to sound self-important, so that when they did present themselves, he always rose to the occasion.

'The sitting-room door was wide open – I remember that quite clearly – and the inspector peered in. The two bedroom doors were closed and I pointed out to him which was Tricia's. He went across and opened it and switched on the light. Then he let out an exclamation of sorts and disappeared inside the room. I remained in the hall near the front-door. When he came out, he asked me in a rather nasty tone why I was standing there and I told him I was merely trying to keep out of his way. I'd already formed the view that he was a somewhat mannerless individual. It was at that point he told me Tricia had been murdered.'

'Did you go into the bedroom yourself?'

'I most certainly did not.'

'How long was Inspector Dormer inside the room and out of your sight?'

167

'Oh dear, what a difficult question to answer! I was scarcely in a state of mind to remember things like that.'

'If you could give me some sort of estimate, it would help.'

'Not a long time,' Norman said with judicial caution. 'On the other hand he didn't just dash in and out. I suppose he was in there for about two minutes.'

'Thank you, Mr Oliver, that's most helpful.'

'But why do you want to know that?' Norman asked in a suddenly suspicious voice.

'I was just testing your recollection of details to see if you'd make a good witness and you've passed with flying colours,' Rosa said blithely.

He was still puzzling over this, however, when she departed a few minutes later.

As she drove back to her own flat, she realised how hungry she was. She'd have a meal as soon as she got in.

It was later while she was making herself an omelette that her thoughts began to crystalise.

If she could prove that Dormer had planted the hair on Tricia's pillow, that would be sufficient to secure Toby's acquittal, as well as ensure the D.I.'s disgrace.

It could then be left to the police to discover who had really committed the murder. She would have achieved what she had set out to do. As she had reminded Robin, counter-attack was the best form of defence, a precept she was out to prove once more.

After finishing her supper, she put through a call to the rectory to find out the latest news of her father. To her surprise, he answered the telephone himself and assured her that, apart from one or two bruises, he was perfectly all right.

Though conscious that she still had much to do before the outcome was even in sight, she felt the day had ended on a better note than it had begun.

CHAPTER 21

Even the most straightforward case involves a prodigious amount of documentation before it ever reaches court. The police take statements not only from those directly caught up in the dramatic happening, but from anyone who might have a relevant word to say. Few of this great host ever get near the witness box.

It was on to the shoulders of Detective Sergeants Speed and Holthouse, assisted by a number of detective constables, that most of this routine work fell after Toby's arrest.

On the next day, which was Tuesday, Sergeant Speed had just returned to his desk after a morning of taking such statements, when his telephone rang.

'Is that Sergeant Speed?' a taut voice asked.

'Hello, Mr Harris. I was about to call you and find out when I could come and take a short statement from you concerning Tricia Langley's employment by your company. Is that what you're ringing me about?'

'No. I'm afraid something extremely worrying has come to light and I'd like to talk to you as soon as possible. At the moment, I just don't know what to think.'

'Does it concern Tricia's death?'

'That'll be for you to judge.'

'I can come right away if you like.'

'I'd be most grateful. I'll be waiting for you.'

Brian Speed let out a sigh as he gazed at the accumulation of paper on his desk. It would just have to gather another layer of dust.

When, half an hour later, he arrived at the company's chic premises, the tall, willowy receptionist greeted him with a faintly awed look and took him immediately to Mr Harris' room.

Giles Harris met him at the door, shook his hand, waved him to a chair and sat down behind his desk like someone in a speeded-up movie.

'It's about Joyce Wyngard,' he said, nervously placing his fingertips together as though making an electrical contact. 'She had an accident on Sunday evening. She was knocked down by a motor cyclist and sustained a broken wrist, as well as various cuts and bruises. She was fairly shaken up I gather and they kept her in hospital for twenty-four hours. That meant she wasn't in the office yesterday. Anyway, to cut a long story, it very much looks as if she's been dipping her hand in the till; or to be rather less euphemistic, that she's embezzled a tidy sum of money. I had occasion to go to her room to look for something and quite accidentally came across an invoice and receipt which aroused my suspicions. I delved further and my worst fears were confirmed.'

'How much has she had?'

'I've no idea; but I have a horrible feeling that what I found was a mere tip of the iceberg. It'll need our accountants to sort it all out.'

'Does she know what you've discovered?'

'I've not told a soul. She phoned me when she got back from hospital yesterday eveɪ ing and said she'd be in today. But I told her there was no poinι if her arm was out of action. She was clearly desperately eager to come in and I had to say that I'd immediately send her home again if she appeared. Of course, I knew by then that her eagerness didn't reflect her conscientiousness so much as her anxiety about what might be discovered in her absence.'

After a few further questions, Brian Speed had an all too familiar picture. That of the faithful employee who arrives early, leaves late and is always reluctant to take a holiday. Such industrious paragons were all too often those who handled their employer's money.

'What makes you believe this has any connection with Tricia's murder?' he asked.

Harris drew a deep breath. 'Joyce has been very nervy of late. Ever since the murder, in fact. I didn't think much about it, because quite frankly I have sufficient other things to occupy my mind. I did vaguely wonder what was her trouble. I knew it couldn't be grief because she and Tricia had never got on. In fact, they raised sparks off each other. Then I suddenly recalled Tricia making a strange and rather snide remark to the effect that the oldest and solidest-looking stones often hid the nastiest maggots. It happened when I had ticked her off for being late two mornings running. I had no idea what she meant and was certainly in no mood to enquire at the time. I'm now wondering, however, if she mayn't have been referring obliquely to Joyce's dishonesty. I even wonder if she may not have been quietly blackmailing her.' He gave Speed a worried look. 'That's where the connection comes in.'

'I'll have to report this to my guvnor,' Speed said, with a sinking heart.

Having just arrested Toby Nash, he couldn't see Superintendent Savill being overjoyed by the news. It was clear, however, that Joyce Wyngard would have to be further interviewed.

After Giles Harris had shown him the documentary evidence of his discovery, Speed departed, with a promise to get in touch again shortly.

Detective Superintendent Savill's reception of the news was as unenthusiastic as Brian Speed had expected.

'She's at home, did you say? Then we'll go and see her now. The sooner this red herring is disposed of, the better.'

'You think it is a red herring, sir?'

'It has to be. Almost the only thing about which Inspector Dormer and I are in agreement is that it wasn't a woman's sort of murder.'

Wait till you've seen Joyce Wyngard, Speed wanted to say. But Savill was obviously not in a mood to brook any argument.

It was a few minutes before seven when Speed rang the bell of her flat, which was on the ground floor of a semi-detached house.

Joyce Wyngard opened the door and stared suspiciously at her visitors. Then she recognised Speed and a flicker of fear

171

showed itself in her eyes. Her right arm was in a sling with the wrist itself encased in plaster.

'This is Detective Superintendent Savill, Miss Wyngard. We'd like to come in and talk to you.'

They followed her into the front room where Speed cast a jaundiced glance at the cat, one of whose hairs he had so carefully taken away on his previous visit.

'There seems to be evidence, Miss Wyngard, that you've been defrauding your employer,' Savill said. 'However, that's a matter which'll be investigated by officers of another division. My only interest is the extent to which it may have provided you with a motive to murder Tricia Langley.'

She gave a gasp. 'I never ... '

'It'd be better if you let me finish before you say anything. I understand that you and Miss Langley weren't on good terms and there's been a suggestion that she had found out what you were doing.'

'I never murdered her,' she said in a harsh whisper.

'Had she found out about your defalcations?'

'She liked taunting me and pretending she knew something about me.'

'Was she blackmailing you?'

'Certainly not!'

'Nevertheless, it could be said that you had a motive for murdering her.'

'I tell you I didn't do it.'

'Weren't you worried that she might suddenly decide to give you away?'

Joyce Wyngard's mouth tightened into a stubborn line.

'I give you my word I didn't kill her,' she said.

'Can you give me something better than that? I need it before I can be satisfied you had nothing to do with the murder.'

'If I'd gone there to kill her, do you think it likely she would have invited me into her bedroom? It would have happened in the sitting-room.'

'You might have followed her into the bedroom when she went to fetch something.'

'I thought she'd been sexually assaulted on the bed.'

172

'That was how it looked, but it could have been faked.'

In a scornful tone, she said, 'I'd never suffocate someone with a pillow. It means a struggle and it takes time.'

Savill gave her a startled look.

'And how would you go about it?' he asked.

'A karate chop to the neck. Swift and painless. That's what I'd use if I was attacked in the street.'

Savill blinked at her in astonishment. 'I think I should advise you to be extremely careful on whom you use your karate chops.' After a reflective pause, he went on, 'When Sergeant Speed spoke to you last week, you told him you were alone at home the whole of the previous Friday evening.'

'Yes.'

'What time did you get back from work?'

'I suppose it would have been around six thirty.'

'And you were at home from then on?'

'Apart from taking my cat to the vet.'

'What time was that?'

'I came in, put him in his basket and went straight out again. I didn't even take my coat off.'

'And what time did you return from the vet.'

'There were a lot of people waiting that evening. It had turned a quarter to eight when I got back.'

'So, between near enough six thirty and a quarter to eight, you were at the vet's.'

'Yes.'

'Why didn't you mention going to the vet to Sergeant Speed?'

'Because he merely asked me where I'd spent the evening and I told him. At home. I didn't regard my visit to the vet as of any significance.'

'It's about the most significant thing you could have told him. May I have his name and address?'

She gave it and added, 'He's only five minutes walk away.'

Shortly afterwards, the two officers departed. As they got into their car, Savill said, 'What a woman! You were right to have uneasy feelings about her, Brian.'

173

'You're satisfied, sir, that she had nothing to do with the murder?'

'Provided the vet supports her times, she has an alibi.' He let out a deep sigh. 'Another suspect off our list. Just. I must confess I had an uncomfortable few minutes in there, bearing in mind we've already charged Nash.'

Speed refrained from comment. His had been the only voice that had spoken against Nash's arrest when Savill had sought the views of Dormer, himself and Peter Holthouse. At that time, the Detective Superintendent had seemed to share his reservations. Brian Speed still retained his.

CHAPTER 22

It was as well that Rosa knew nothing of the Wyngard development when she set off to visit Miss Greenwood that same Tuesday evening. If she had, she might have been tempted to alter course and go and see her instead, for, on the face of things, she provided the more fertile source of information.

When she had phoned the blind occupant of Flat 3, Miss Greenwood had been polite but distant and had shown no eagerness to be visited. Rosa, however, had been at her most persuasive and eventually Miss Greenwood had agreed, admitting to being intrigued to meet a female lawyer with such a young voice.

She espied nosy Norm as she mounted the steps to the front door, though he appeared to back hastily away when he recognised her.

Rosa had come across a number of blind people in her professional life and had never failed to admire their courage and their refusal to be defeated by such an enormous handicap. It didn't take her long to realise that Miss Greenwood belonged to the same sturdily self-reliant group.

'It's a very personal question,' the blind woman said after they had been talking for a short time, 'but how old are you?'

'Twenty-eight. Is that what I sound?'

Miss Greenwood chuckled. 'Anyone in their twenties ought to sound young. I'd very much like to have been a lawyer myself, but it was not to be.'

'There are a number of blind solicitors,' Rosa said hesitantly.

'Oh, it had nothing to do with being blind. It was a question of money. In those days, there weren't all the grants which are now available to students. In any event, I didn't go blind until I was nineteen. It was the result of a serious illness.'

'That must be even worse than being born blind. To have known sight and to have lost it must be cruel.'

'The worst part was when my sight was failing. One day hopes of saving it would be raised, only to be shattered the next. Once it had irrevocably happened, I could at least start adjusting to it. And believe me, Miss Epton, I still have much for which to be thankful. But it isn't my blindness that has brought you here, so now it's your turn to talk while I listen.'

There was a moment's silence while Rosa assembled her thoughts and Miss Greenwood sat as still as a tree on a windless day.

'I'm defending the person charged with Tricia Langley's murder. He's a young man named Toby Nash. He strenuously denies having done it and though I don't usually express belief in my clients' innocence, in this instance I am convinced that the police have made a ghastly mistake.' She noticed a tiny smile flicker across Miss Greenwood's face and wondered if the blind woman had divined her emotional involvement in the case. 'My object in coming to see you is to find out if you heard anything that Friday evening when Tricia was killed which might assist me in undoing a terrible wrong.'

'I've already told the police all I can. Or very nearly all. I certainly heard a man's footsteps overhead between seven and seven thirty that evening and I later heard him come downstairs. I didn't hear a single further sound from the flat above during the rest of the weekend.

'As I told the police, I had the distinct impression of having heard the same footsteps on an earlier occasion. Some days or even a week before that Friday.' She gave Rosa a small amused smile. 'You see, my ears, which also have to serve as my eyes, have become attuned to distinguishing sounds.'

'When did the police first interview you, Miss Greenwood?'

'On the Sunday evening. They were in the house when my cousin brought me back from church. The street was full of comings and goings as we drove up to the door and we wondered what had happened. Little did we dream there had

176

been a murder. A pleasant young sergeant was waiting to talk to me as I walked in.'

'You said just now that you had told the police all you could and then you added, or very nearly all.'

'That's right. You see I'm almost certain I heard those same footsteps again yesterday morning.' She paused. 'In fact, I'm quite certain.'

'Coming from Flat 4?'

'Yes.'

'That's very, very interesting,' Rosa said in a thoughtful voice. 'I wonder whose they could have been.' As she spoke, she recalled Janice having told her the previous evening that the police had paid an unheralded visit that morning and that nosy Norm had let them into the flat. 'So that was the third time you'd heard those same footsteps.'

'The third, yes.'

'Are you familiar with Mr Oliver's footsteps?'

She made a slight grimace.

'Very familiar,' she said drily.

'Might they have been his?' Rosa asked, and held her breath.

'They were nothing at all like his. Mind you, I frequently do recognise his footsteps overhead. In fact, he was up there yesterday morning when I heard these others. The footsteps I'm referring to were made by a solid pair of shoes. Mr Oliver pads about the house in a pair of slippers.'

It was at that precise moment Rosa suddenly saw the whole monstrous picture in startling clarity.

She knew she must talk to Robin as soon as possible and she prayed that he would be at home that evening.

There was a telephone kiosk at the end of Fillery Street and she parked the car nearby. There was a fat woman making a call and Rosa's heart sank when she saw the pile of coins beside her. She could be talking for hours.

However, even while she was wondering impatiently where there was another public telephone, the woman banged down

177

the receiver, scooped up her unused money and emerged, giving Rosa an angry glare as she waddled away.

Robin, with wife Jean and three children, lived about fifteen miles out of London on its west side. Thanks to the M4, he had less than half an hour's drive from door to door.

To Rosa's intense relief, he answered the phone himself and at once agreed to her driving down to see him.

'I've just finished washing up the supper things,' he said. 'Jean's gone off to a church council meeting and by the time you get here, the children will either be in bed or glued to the box, so we shan't be disturbed.'

She arrived to find he had coffee waiting for her in the sitting-room. On the phone, she had merely said she would like to see him urgently about a new development in the Nash case. He hadn't asked any questions, but as soon as she stepped inside the lighted hall, he saw that she was in a state of pent-up excitement. Her eyes were shining with the brightness of a magician's.

He handed her a cup of coffee and sat down facing her.

'So what's happened?' he asked. 'Obviously something dramatic from all the signs.'

'I now know who murdered Tricia Langley,' she said.

When she finished telling him of her visit to Miss Greenwood, followed by her own reconstruction of how the murder had been accomplished, she sat back in her chair with a look of exhaustion.

Robin, who had listened without interruption, now stared across the room in deep thought.

'It all hinges on Miss Greenwood's identification of someone by their footsteps,' he said slowly. 'I'm not doubting her ability, but I'm trying to see it from the other side. Before we make any move, we must be absolutely sure that we can't be faulted.'

'Obviously it'll be up to the police to clinch the case. I'm not able to do that,' Rosa said with a faint note of impatience.

If Robin observed it, he took no notice. 'I know now what's bothering me,' he said with a frown. 'You say Miss Greenwood heard the footsteps three times in all. But surely he was there four times. The first time would have been when he went to give

178

Tricia a pep talk about turning up and giving evidence. The second would have been the evening of the murder, the third on Sunday evening and the fourth yesterday when he called at the flat with other officers. They must have been on their way there when you saw them in the car as you left court.'

'That's absolutely right, Robin,' she said keenly, 'but you're forgetting that Miss Greenwood was at church on Sunday evening and only returned home when, as she put it, there were all manner of police comings and goings. It's almost certain that Dormer had left by then and was on his way to Swiss Cottage to scare the wits out of Toby.'

'I've known some cold, ruthless types, but nothing to touch Detective Inspector Dormer. To pretend to discover a murder which you've committed yourself and then, with the utmost calculation, set about pinning it on an innocent person ... It's quite unbelievably wicked.'

'To my mind, the really devilish bit of cunning was in that Sunday evening visit. He knew that if the murder had been discovered earlier, he'd have been informed, so he decided to discover it himself and pretend he had gone to the flat to keep an appointment to interview Tricia.'

'When, in fact, that had been Friday evening?'

'Exactly.'

'Would it have been on Sunday that he planted Toby's hair on the pillow?'

'I'm sure it was then.'

'But supposing the murder had already been discovered, he wouldn't have been able to do that.'

'He'd have found some other way of incriminating Toby.'

'If you're right, it couldn't have been a premeditated murder.'

'I don't believe it was. He went there on Friday evening with the intention of bullying her into giving her evidence. She rebuffed him, angry words were exchanged and he completely lost his temper and killed her.'

'What were they doing in the bedroom?'

'I've given that a lot of thought. I don't believe he was seriously intending to rape her. I think it's more likely he

179

followed her when she went in there for some reason or another, she told him to get out and it was then the whole pot boiled over. It's a fact that nobody could be more disdainful and more infuriating than Tricia when she clambered on to her high horse.'

Robin nodded slowly and appeared to lapse into further deep thought.

'Do you agree I should go and lay it all before Savill tomorrow morning?' Rosa asked, breaking in on his silence.

'No.'

'But I must, Robin. I can't just do nothing.'

'Of course you can't. But Savill's compromised himself by charging Toby with the murder. It wouldn't be fair on him and you couldn't expect him to give you an unbiassed hearing.' He paused for a moment. 'I think the best course will be for me to call Dick Weston and ask if you and I can go and see him on a matter of great urgency. I'm certain he'll agree.'

Rosa had met Dick Weston once at a dinner party given by the Snaiths. He was a deputy assistant commissioner at Scotland Yard and a long-standing friend of Robin's.

She let out a heartfelt sigh. 'Thanks, Robin,' she said with a grateful smile. 'I was worried you might think I'd finally succumbed to paranoia.'

CHAPTER 23

Two days later several things happened which set all Inspector Dormer's alarm bells ringing.

On returning from lunch somewhat earlier than usual, he discovered that his official diary was missing from the drawer in which he always kept it. He searched the other drawers of his desk and then looked beneath the files and paper that littered the top, but to no avail.

He sat back in his chair in a thoughtful mood. Eventually he was forced to conclude that it had been removed deliberately. Moreover, the fact that it had been taken without his permission or knowledge could fill him only with foreboding.

All along he had been aware that his official diary could become a time bomb. His pocketbook and the station occurrence book were records which were completed after an event had taken place, but the diary bore testimony to the future. Hence there had been a fateful entry for Friday, 11th January which had read: *7 p.m. T. Langley, 52 Fillery St.*

His pocket book and the occurrence book were silent as to his activities that evening, but the diary had become a damning piece of evidence.

In the end, he had decided the best thing to do was to excise the offending page as neatly as he could and interleave one for the same day that he had removed from a diary issued to one of his detective constables who had been on sick leave since Christmas. He knew that any attempt to obliterate or erase the entry would be an invitation to awkward questions. As it was, provided it wasn't being examined with suspicions already alerted, there was every chance the substituted page would pass unremarked.

On the other hand, if someone's attention was focussed on that particular page, it was bound to be detected.

With the diary missing in what he could only regard as suspicious circumstances, he felt obliged to face the unpalatable fact that somewhere along the line he had made a fatal slip. His thoughts at once flew to Rosa. Well, she would quickly discover that he still had a vicious sting in his tail.

He was grimly considering what to do when a uniformed chief inspector came into his room and asked him for his pocketbook.

'The Super's got nothing better to do this afternoon, so he's decided to inspect all pocketbooks,' he said with spurious bonhomie.

Dormer handed it to him, but didn't deign to comment on such a transparent deception.

It was about an hour later that Superintendent Savill came on the line.

'Can you meet me at the flat in Fillery Street about four o'clock?' he asked. 'I want to have another look around for evidence which'll strengthen our case against Nash and I'd be glad if you'd come along and help.'

This time the scent of danger was so strong that Dormer knew he was being invited to walk into a trap.

''Fraid not,' he said laconically.

'I wouldn't ask you if it wasn't important,' Savill said in a faintly nonplussed voice.

'I've set up a vital meeting with an informant this evening and can't break it. He's expecting me about that time.'

'Treacherous bastard!' Dormer muttered to himself as Savill rang off.

He continued to brood over events and, in particular, to try and identify the slip he must have made.

When, shortly before he left to go and meet his imaginary informant, he received a curt message requiring his attendance at divisional headquarters at nine the next morning, he knew he was facing a crisis.

As soon as he reached home that evening, he fetched from its cupboard the typewriter which belonged to his sister. Inserting a sheet of headed paper he had taken from the magistrates' court, he began typing. On this occasion, his two fingers hit the

182

keys not only viciously, but with a venom that matched the content of his missive.

He read through what he had written with malicious satisfaction. All he now had to decide was when to post it. That still depended on events.

But when it did reach its destination, he had every hope it would destroy Rosa Epton's career beneath an avalanche of public humiliation.

As the evening wore on, he brooded more and more on what would have been sprung on him, had he gone to Fillery Street at Savill's request. He felt certain he was to have been confronted with something, while his reaction was closely watched. It must be something that told against him. But what? It was a question which nagged him like an aching tooth.

Suddenly he reached a decision. If Savill could be devious, so could he. He would ring the flat and make a pretext for going there, subject to certain precautions. It was only just after eight o'clock, so nothing untoward could be seen in his visit.

He dialled the number and Sara answered.

'It's Detective Inspector Dormer, Miss Fitch,' he said in a considerably more genial tone than he usually adopted. 'Have any of my colleagues been in touch with you today?'

'Not as far as I'm concerned.'

'As we work from different stations, I wasn't sure. In that event, I'd like to come round within the next hour and make a further check on Miss Langley's room.'

'But some of your lot did that only a few days ago.'

'I know. This is a follow-up.'

'All right,' Sara said with reluctance. 'I'll be here, but Janice is out.'

'As long as there's someone to let me in,' he said.

He arrived about half an hour later and managed to get into the house without arousing the landlord's interest. Sara admitted him to the flat and he went at once into Tricia's bedroom, closing the door behind him.

It was at least five minutes before he joined her in the

sitting-room, where he began pacing up and down in a strangely nervous manner.

'Did you find what you were looking for?' Sara asked.

He shook his head and fixed her with a troubled look. 'For reasons I'll explain later, Miss Fitch, I shall be glad if you don't mention my visit to Superintendent Savill, should he get in touch with you again. We've had a minor difference of opinion about the conduct of the investigation and he might have it in for me if he knew I'd been here this evening.'

Before Sara could say anything, however, the telephone rang and she went out into the hall to answer it.

'It's Amy Greenwood, dear. Forgive me for being inquisitive, but I believe you have a visitor with you?'

'Detective Inspector Dormer's here.'

'Thank you, dear, that's all I wanted to know. I'll explain later.'

Puzzled by Miss Greenwood's conspiratorial tone, Sara returned to the sitting-room.

'Who was that?' Dormer asked suspiciously.

'It was only Miss Greenwood in the flat below. Ever since Tricia's death she gets fussed when she knows one of us is up here on her own. She was just phoning to make sure everything was all right.'

This was in no sense true, but Sara was embarrassed both by the direct nature of the question and by her own inability to explain why Miss Greenwood had wanted to find out who was with her. Even so she was totally unprepared for Inspector Dormer's reaction.

'It's a bloody trap after all,' he said furiously as he plunged from the room, leaving her staring after him in bewilderment.

She heard him dash downstairs and the front door slam, after which there was an eerie silence.

Meanwhile, in the flat below, Miss Greenwood was dialling Rosa's number.

Dormer drove home with his mind in a turmoil. He felt like an animal caught in a net and struggling to get out. He realised that those investigating him might not now wait till the next morning before manifesting themselves.

He parked his car outside the house and went in.

'Anybody phoned or been round?' he shouted out to his sister who was in the kitchen.

'Nobody.'

He went back outside again. There was one thing he was going to do while he still had time. Post that letter.

CHAPTER 24

As soon as they were satisfied that the wrong man had been charged with Tricia's murder, the police arranged for Toby's immediate release on bail. Then on the day of his next appearance at Fulham Magistrates' Court, a representative of the Director of Public Prosecutions Department turned up and in a deftly tuned piece of advocacy asked for Toby to be discharged, without a stain on his character.

So for the second time in a single month Toby found himself leaving a court a free man.

Rosa was waylaid by Superintendent Savill as she was departing.

'I'm very sorry indeed, Miss Epton, that your client was the object of such a gross injustice. I hope he won't bear any lasting grudge against the police in general. He certainly owes a great deal to you, as I do.' He assumed a rueful expression. 'My trouble was that I was blind to the possibility of the Metropolitan Police nurturing in its ranks a man quite so evil as Inspector Dormer. I still find it difficult to comprehend.'

'You wouldn't if you'd had him up against you as I have.'

'Probably not. I remember being surprised, and even rather shocked, by his vindictiveness toward you and Nash the first time he and I met on the case.' He sighed. 'I'm not making excuses, but, in a sense, I was pushed into charging Nash.'

'I don't bear you any ill feelings, Mr Savill, and I doubt whether Toby Nash will.'

'I'm grateful for those words.'

'I'm surprised that Dormer didn't flee the country when he had the opportunity.'

'I think that's partly explained by his general lack of imagination. He hadn't made any contingency plans to skip. Apart from the fact he never expected to be found out, I'm told that he detests all foreigners and has only once been abroad in his life and that was when he was in the army in Germany during the fifties. So, abroad to him wouldn't have been a very inviting prospect, even if it meant avoiding prison in his own country. In any event, we shouldn't have rested until we'd located him and got him back. Extradition or no extradition! Nevertheless I'm glad we've been saved that trouble and already have him safely locked up.'

It was a few evenings later that Rosa and Toby went out for a second celebratory dinner.

'We'll go to a different restaurant this time,' Toby had said firmly.

He picked her up at her flat and gave her an admiring look when she opened the door.

'I've come straight from home,' he said with a grin. 'I didn't stop off to murder anyone on the way.'

He hadn't told Rosa where they were going so that she blinked in surprise when they pulled up outside a very expensive French restaurant in Chelsea.

'Here?' she said.

'I thought the occasion called for somewhere special.'

'You'll need a bank loan to pay the bill.'

'Incidentally, I've told my bank it can stuff itself. I'm not going back.' After they had been shown to their table and handed menus he went on, 'One thing about prison is it gives you lots of time to think. And I thought a great deal. For me, that is. Anyway, I've decided to go back to Australia.'

'Back?'

'Yes, didn't I ever mention it? I spent a couple of years there in my early twenties. I only came home because my mother was dying. I liked the people and the way of life there.' He smiled at her. 'Life here has become too fraught and I can hardly expect you to go on getting me out of Brixton. Twice is enough. Also, this is the moment to make a break.'

'You know you'll be required to give evidence against Dormer,' Rosa said. 'And his trial's not likely to come on for months.'

'It'll give me the greatest pleasure when the time comes.

187

Witnesses get all their expenses paid, don't they?' Rosa nodded. 'So that's all right. I'll send you my address and keep in touch.'

While Toby was ordering, she wondered why she had been unaware of his previous stay in Australia until it dawned on her that he rarely mentioned the past. The present and the immediate future were the frontiers of Toby's world, which accounted for his remarkably buoyant nature.

'That was a wonderful dinner,' Rosa said with a contented sigh as the waiter brought them their coffee.

'I hope Inspector Dormer enjoyed his mug of cocoa,' Toby said cheerfully. 'I like to picture him occupying my old cell.'

Rosa gave an abstracted nod. Her mind was temporarily elsewhere. It was that day she had learnt of the letter Dormer had written to the Law Society about her. She had a copy in her bag, but suddenly decided not to show it to Toby, as she had intended. What was the point?

He drove her home and stopped outside her block of flats. Then he gave her a sidelong glance and Rosa knew very well what he was thinking.

'Don't bother to switch off the engine,' she said quickly.

Leaning over, she kissed him lightly on the lips before jumping out and hurrying inside the building.

Though she would undoubtedly see him again before he left and when he returned to give evidence at Dormer's trial, she felt the evening marked the end of a relationship. A relationship that had stretched both her mind and her emotions.

When she got upstairs, she took the letter out of her bag and, with a set expression, read it through again.

Dear Sir, (it ran)

I think you should have it on official record that, according to my information, Rosa Epton of Snaith and Epton was co-habiting with her client, Toby Nash, at the very time she was defending him on a serious rape charge in this court. Such scandalous conduct should not, I feel, be allowed to go unpublicised.

Yours Truly

(the signature was illegible)

Chairman of Petersham Magistrates Court.

Robin, who had spoken to an official at the Law Society, had been assured that now the full circumstances were known to them, nothing would stand against her name. The same official had regretted the defamation which had ensued when the society, acting in all good faith, had followed up the complaint. It was now seen, he had added severely, as a malicious, mischief-making document.

But, as Rosa well knew, the harm done by such a letter was not lightly undone.

'I'm afraid you'll just have to live with it until it passes into the mists of time,' Robin had said philosophically, adding, 'In these tumultuous days, that won't be long.'

She was glad now that she hadn't shown it to Toby as she doubted whether he would have understood how bitter she felt about it. To him, it would have been something you shrugged off and cast into the rubbish bin into which all disagreeable experiences were consigned.

She had just put it away in a drawer of her desk, when the telephone rang.

It was a few minutes before midnight and she wondered who could be phoning her at that hour. Could her father have had another fall? Or was it Toby pleading loneliness?

She lifted the receiver warily and at once heard Philippa's unmistakable tones.

'Rosa, darling, you're simply never in. I've been trying to get you for days. I'm dying to hear what's been going on, so when will you come to dinner? Now that we've met up again, we mustn't lose touch. It seems ages since I saw you ... not since my New Year's Eve party.'